Batting Cleanup (Tag & Skye Part 3)

A Columbia Gems Baseball Romance

MJ Compton

BATTING CLEANUP (TAG & SKYE PART 3)

The publisher does not have any control over and does not assume any responsibility for author or third-party websites or their content.

This book was previously published as MASK OF THE QUEEN

Original Release Date: March 7, 2017

DEDICATION

To Central New York Romance Writers. Without my local RWA chapter I never could have written this story.

Acknowledgments

To The Purples: Carol Lombardo, Christine Wenger, Gayle, Callen, and Kris Fletcher. "Never give up! Never surrender!"

Author note: Since this book was originally written and published, the rules of baseball have changes. Any errors are my own.

CONTENTS

WEDNESDAY, MARCH 1

"You're not Jewish?" Joel Green, the new director of Columbia's Jewish Community Center, eyed Celeste "Skye" Schuyler with suspicion.

"Nope." Skye forced her cheeriness. "But I do have my kosher certification. I explained all this to your predecessor when he signed the contract for me to cater the Purim Carnival."

She kept her smile firmly in place. Didn't even grit her teeth.

"Kosher is more than no lobster or bacon." The poor man was truly distressed.

"I know. Don't worry. My certification is legitimate. And I'm a vegan caterer, too. The two cuisines work well together."

He didn't seem assured. "Why would you cater kosher meals if you're not Jewish?"

"I like to cook. I like studying various cuisines. I saw a need for a kosher caterer in Columbia. It was a business decision."

She didn't know what her religious or cultural orientation had to do with her ability to cook kosher. Yes, she understood *kashrut*—the dietary laws—wasn't the same as being able to cook Thai or French. But the secondary kitchen in her Skye's The Limit building had been certified kosher. She had completely separate cooking utensils. She understood what she could and couldn't do. In fact, she'd already catered a wedding reception at one of the local synagogues. Her credentials had been scrutinized by the previous director of the JCC before he signed the contract for her to cater the Purim Carnival.

Green finally smiled at her, but the ice in his vivid blue eyes didn't melt. "Given the current political climate, you have to understand why the center is being cautious."

She'd heard about the rise in hate crimes around the country. She couldn't escape it. Especially when she was a victim, too.

"Nothing has happened here, has it?" she asked.

"There was a threat back in January. And the Purim Carnival is the first big event we've had this calendar year, so it's...attractive. We'll be beefing up security as well as taking a closer look at all our vendors."

He was trying to tell her his questions weren't personal. "Completely understandable."

Skye really needed this job. She'd signed the contract the previous autumn, right after her certification had come through. She'd been scrambling then, trying to come up with a balloon payment on her mortgage. Then the local baseball team won the National League pennant and went to the World Series. Since her contract with the Columbia Gems called for her to cater all home games, she'd gotten four unexpected but quite welcome jobs from the series.

Catering jobs weren't the only thing she'd gotten.

"And frankly, something came up in our background check on you that concerns us."

Skye's stomach dropped, probably along with her blood pressure. She knew what was coming.

"Tag Gentry," Green said.

Tag Gentry. The Columbia Gems catcher whose play at the plate during the final game of the National League pennant race had put the Gems in the World Series. Who'd sacrificed his leg for his team. Who had become Skye's friend with benefits when the team hired her to feed him during his initial rehab. Who she'd had the complete lack of common sense to fall in love with.

Yeah. That guy.

Thanks to his jealous ex, the world believed Skye had exposed him as a steroid user. That she'd betrayed him. That she was untrustworthy.

She waited for Green to explain, while he seemed to be waiting for a response from her.

Her relationship with Tag was no one's business but hers and Tag's. Nor did it have any bearing on her ability to cook a kugel.

Actually, she wished she knew what her relationship with Tag was. Because it *was* her business. But Tag was getting weird, and Skye decided the most important thing she could do was protect her heart. Because she'd done the world's stupidest thing by falling in love with the man.

The clock on Green's desk ticked loudly in the ensuing silence. Did he think all he had to do was mention a name and she'd start talking?

He broke first. "You do know Tag Gentry."

"Of course." Everybody in Columbia knew who Tag Gentry was. "He's the catcher for the Gems who broke his leg last year."

Green steepled his fingers. Skye sat back in her chair. Yes, she needed the job, but she wasn't going to let anyone intimidate her. She was through being a wimp. Especially to a man.

As a child, her father had dragged her around the country, always looking for something better, something that didn't exist for him. Drake Dixon, majority shareholder of the Columbia Gems, tried to mess with her mortgage, not to mention her body. When he didn't get away with that, he tried to destroy her career. And maybe he'd succeeded. Based on this conversation, she was going to add Joel Green's name to her shit list.

"And you know that. Otherwise you wouldn't have asked." Skye crossed her legs and jiggled her foot. "Now, I appreciate your concern. After all, I'm going to be at the festival, and the hate crimes worry me too. But I'm also a little offended that you assume because I'm not Jewish I can't cook kosher and that I might be a threat."

She was still raw from New Orleans, where she'd been contracted to cater a Mardi Gras party. To say Mardi Gras had been a nightmare was like saying the Pope was Catholic. Drake Dixon had lured her to the French Quarter to finish what Tag had prevented at Halloween.

"Look," Green said. "Purim is a very festive, happy holiday for us. It commemorates the thwarting of a plot by the government to kill the Jews."

"They tried to kill us. They couldn't. Let's eat." Skye smiled as she repeated an old joke.

Green's lips tightened. "It's easy to joke when you're not in the crosshairs."

"You're right. I apologize. I guess it wasn't my joke to make."

"We're especially vulnerable during Purim," Green continued after a moment. "We're supposed to get so drunk we can't tell the hero from the villain of the Purim story. Although we don't have alcohol at our festival. It's more family oriented. But there's a giddiness involved, as well as costumes and masks."

"Masks?" Skye heard her voice squeak. She inhaled deeply. This wasn't a free-for-all like Mardi Gras. Nor was it a private party for a letch like the Halloween fiasco at Drake Dixon's. Purim Carnival was a family event. Children. Events for children. Foods children would eat.

"I'm going with a meat menu," Skye said. Talking business helped her regain control. "Grilled hot dogs. Kosher, of course. Mini knish—potato and kasha. I have already started baking several kinds of hamantaschen." She needed to show this man she was prepared. That she knew what she was doing.

"Apricot?" he asked.

She smiled. All the world loved a cookie and hamantaschen was a favorite with this crowd. "Of course. And prune, strawberry, and chocolate. Dark chocolate—no milk. People will be able to eat them with their hot dogs." Mixing dairy products and meat was forbidden by dietary laws, and it didn't hurt to let him know she knew it. "And I have some other holiday-themed ideas. I have done my research, Mr. Green. I know the basic story of the two queens, the villain, the king, and Uncle Mordechai. I won't embarrass you, me, or the Jewish community."

The lock on the back door of the once-abandoned restaurant Skye was converting into her catering headquarters stuck. She'd been meaning to have it replaced for months. She leaned against the heavy wooden panel, which aligned the tumblers so she could insert her key. Jiggled said key. Unlocked the door. God forbid she ever try to get inside in a hurry.

Like now. She took her time. There was no rush. She'd purposely blanked her mind after the meeting with Joel Green. Otherwise she might have driven her van into a telephone pole.

Drake Dixon was facing charges for illegal gambling, but the damage he'd done to her reputation would haunt her for the rest of her days. People believed she'd found out Tag was taking steroids and she'd leaked it to the press. She was scum.

There were two camps: Tag's steroid use was none of her business so she should have kept her mouth shut, or the folk who thought she should have dealt with her discovery through team management at the least or the National League at the most. No matter that Tag wasn't doping and that she hadn't sent anyone an e-mail about it. Drake Dixon had rigged it so both Tag and Skye's names were smeared in scandal.

Skye slipped off her jacket and hung it in the closet, then filled her teakettle and put it on the burner. The binder containing her plans for the Purim Carnival sat on the butcher-block island, mocking her. This should have been a fun job.

She'd been to several planning meetings once her contract had been signed. She'd missed a couple of sessions because the Gems had called her down to Florida to cook for spring training. The committee secretary had been e-mailing the notes to Skye so she could be on top of things. No surprises.

The event was to be a fun day for every age. Face painting and bouncy rides for children, klezmer bands—Jewish jazz, she'd been told—for the older folks, a Purim Spiel, which was a play about the biblical book of Esther, which in turn was the story of Purim. Loud and rowdy. Bright daylight. No murky corners or torch-lit tableaux. She'd been really looking forward to being part of something that sounded so joyous.

The teakettle whistled. She poured the boiling water into her favorite oversized yellow mug and dropped in an herbal tea bag that was supposed to tame tension. Hers, it seemed, might require a chair and a whip.

Her phone pinged. She'd changed her ring tones since she'd returned to Columbia from New Orleans, and wasn't sure who was calling. The screen told her it was Tag. The last person in the world she wanted to talk to. It was probably a booty call. Two months ago, she might have been too eager to answer. Now she was at the other end of the spectrum. She didn't want her booty being called. She didn't want the benefits of being Tag Gentry's friend. Staying in their relationship would only make things worse when it finally ended, and she knew that eventually it would end. Tag Gentry was an adventurer. A thrill seeker. The only reason he'd looked twice at her was because she was there in his hour of need, with the team hiring her to cater his meals while he was wheelchair-bound. Friends. Benefits.

And look where it had got her. She'd been trying to leave town with the packing slip for steroids someone had allegedly shipped to him and instead she'd been robbed. Now both of their names were smeary with Dixon doo. Maybe Tag's ex, reporter Terra Baldwin, had filed the story with the Internet website, but Drake Dixon was behind her actions. Once Dixon had been arrested for illegal gambling, Skye had learned he'd been blackmailing Noah Nash, which was how both she and Tag had ended up in New Orleans at Mardi Gras. Skye was certain Dixon had something on Terra, too, but she didn't care enough to want to know what.

So Skye ignored Tag's call. She dunked her tea bag in the water. The repetitive action was soothing. The aroma of spearmint and chamomile filled the kitchen. She'd held herself together between the JCC and Skye's the Limit. Now she could fall apart and wallow in being an emotional mess. In many ways, she was past due for a meltdown.

She'd just taken her first sip of the still-scalding tea when someone rapped on the kitchen door. Hot liquid splashed over her hand when she started at the sound.

No one ever knocked on her door. The last person who'd done that...was Drake Dixon, back in October. Very few people even knew where she was located. No lights shone in the front of the building. The kitchen door led to an alley, where at night a lone security light struggled to penetrate the darkness. But although it was still afternoon, she had no way to verify who was at the door. The broken doorbell was on her list of repairs still needed, but it wasn't nearly as important as some of the other things the building required.

"Red, it's me." And the pounding renewed.

Damn it. Tag had never shown up at Skye's the Limit before.

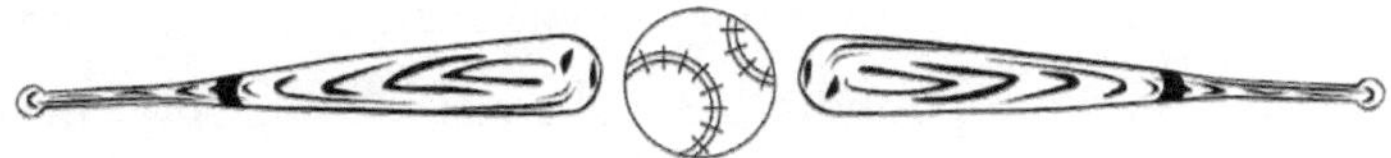

Tucker Alexander Gentry, known throughout the sporting world as Tag, had had just about enough of Celeste "Skye" Schuyler's nonsense and then some. She'd been eluding him since they'd gotten off the plane the previous afternoon. They were supposed to be engaged to be married. She was not merely avoiding him but ignoring him. Tag was not the kind of man who took kindly to be disregarded.

Which was why he was standing in a stinking narrow alley pounding on the back door of Skye's the Limit in the middle of a dreary, rainy afternoon.

Her old white van was parked there, so he knew she was around. The van was her only vehicle. He knew, too, that she lived above the catering premises, in an apartment that had yet to be rehabbed. Knowing Red, that probably meant water-stained plaster hanging from the ceilings in crumbling strips, rodent-chewed electrical wires, and a sleeping bag on the floor.

One of the things he most admired about Red was her tenacity and her determination to make a success of her catering business.

Except when it came to her determination to pay no attention to him. He'd asked her to marry him. A woman didn't simply ignore a proposal. Unless she was nuts. And Red wasn't nuts.

He used his fist on the door. Maybe she was upstairs and couldn't hear him pounding. But she refused to answer her phone. Text messages. E-mails. She'd left him no choice.

The door swung open, and he was faced with the most beautiful sight he'd ever seen. Red's copper-wire curls were unrestrained and wild. Her lagoon-colored eyes were stormy. And she had no idea how stunning she appeared.

"What do you want?" The exasperation in her voice matched the expression in her eyes.

He was the one who should be fed up with her game playing. "You aren't answering your phone."

"I'm busy."

"Aren't you going to ask me in?" He'd already inserted his left foot between the door and the jamb.

Red scrubbed her face with her palms. "Didn't we spend enough time together in New Orleans? I need a break."

New Orleans. Now there had been a disaster. "I proposed to you in New Orleans," he reminded her.

"I rest my case."

She started to close the door, but he was too quick, despite his bad leg.

"I get the feeling we're not on the same page here," he said, as he forced his way into her space. He looked around, taking mental note of the kitchen. Her new used stove, not the outrageously expensive one she wanted. Butcher block and granite counters. Intense overhead lighting to make up for a lack of windows.

"Look, I just had a really crappy meeting. Okay? I don't need any attitude from you." She flounced to the center island and perched on a stool. A lone mug sat on the wooden surface, its contents steaming.

Tag sat opposite her. He liked hanging with her. This kitchen, with its exposed brick walls, suited her. She was wearing his favorite teal sweater, which enhanced the color of her eyes and molded her breasts the way he liked his hands to cup her.

"What's wrong?" he asked. He knew he'd have to pry her problems out of her. That was just the way she was. Private. Not secretive—just not forthcoming with all her business.

"I told you about the event I'm doing for the JCC," she said. "I met with the new director today, and he's not comfortable that I'm not Jewish."

"You're not Japanese either, but you make a mean California roll."

She picked up her cup and drank, peering at him over the yellow rim the entire time. Then she set the mug on the counter. "That's not quite it. They have concerns over security. Hate crimes have increased over the past several months."

"What does that have to do with you?" Anyone who thought Red was a hater needed their head examined.

She hesitated. "Nothing. They're just concerned. Do you want something to drink?"

"I'm good. So when are we going shopping?" No point beating around the bush.

"Shopping?" A vee formed between her eyebrows. "For what?"

"A ring. A diamond ring. You know, to formalize our engagement."

Red stared at him for several seconds before answering. "You're not serious."

"I'm completely serious. I do not joke about things like my freedom."

"Come on. You know I said I'd marry you just to get out of New Orleans in one piece."

Her voice cracked. Hairline fracture.

Something else was going on with her. And he didn't like her casual attitude. He'd been serious about marriage. Yeah, it bothered him that she apparently didn't care about him the way he did her. "I guess I didn't get the memo," he grumbled.

Maybe it was time to start dating her, but what did people do on dates? He felt funny asking her out to dinner, because she was an amazing cook. Baseball season was still several weeks away, and he wasn't sure he wanted to go to the ballpark if he couldn't play. A movie? He'd never understood why someone would go to the movies on a first date. They weren't like a baseball game, where you could talk but still follow the action on the field.

He'd never had to come up with ideas before. He was Tag Gentry. Women asked him out, and by out, they usually meant to bed. What else was there besides dinner, baseball games, and movies? It wasn't as if he could ski, either on snow or the water. He might be able to manage miniature golf. If he had a cart and actually knew how to play, he could golf. The idea intrigued him. He'd played some in high school. A ball. A club or a bat. Green grass.

"So you don't want to go shopping. Fine. What about a movie?"

"No, but thanks." She took another sip from her mug. "I'm so tired, I'd probably fall asleep."

"What do you like to do?" he asked.

Red started. "What do you mean?"

"For fun. What do you do for fun?"

"I cook. I try new recipes. I read."

"No. For fun. Cooking and recipes and reading are work."

"No. I like to read. Historical romance novels."

Tag didn't know what to say to that. Reading was something he'd done to get through high school so he could play ball.

"You don't hike or swim or jog?" He couldn't imagine a life without movement. Without action.

Red wrinkled her nose. "No. I told you before. My father moved me around a lot when I was a kid. I'm all for staying put."

If he was going to date her, get to know her, he had to figure out something. She wasn't helping at all. "Well, what do you want to do?"

"I want to finish my tea and work on my plans for the Purim Carnival."

"The what?"

"The job I have for the JCC. Every year, they have a carnival in their gym. It's one of the Jewish holidays."

"How did you get that job?"

"I pitched them after I got my kosher certification. Why?"

"It just seems like a strange thing for you to do."

"If you think that, then you don't know me at all."

"Not for lack of trying," he muttered.

But that wasn't quite true. Their relationship to this point had been about him. Red taking care of him. Watching out for him. Oh, he'd been able to stop Drake Dixon's attempted rape of her, maybe even twice. But of all the hours they'd spent in each other's company, most of them had been about him. Or sex.

Sex was good. He nearly always wanted sex. Especially when the sex was with Red. But there hadn't been much of that lately either. Nor was he sure he could maneuver two flights of stairs to her apartment. So unless she was willing to head out to his penthouse in a much nicer part of the city, there probably wouldn't be any sex today.

He eyed the counter. Too high, unless he leaned her over it, and even then, he figured she might protest about how unsanitary fucking in her kitchen would be.

"So you want to grab a bite to eat?" Okay, he was desperate.

"What is up with you?" she asked. "Why are you acting so weird?"

"What's so weird about asking you out?"

"We hang. We have sex. We don't go out."

"Well, maybe we should."

"Why?"

"To get to know each other."

"We know each other just fine."

"Yeah? What's my favorite color?"

"Columbia Gem teal. Like my sweater."

Yeah. Of course she knew that. She'd gotten him a cane with teal pinstriping on it. He'd really liked the cane. But it had been stolen and destroyed in New Orleans.

"What's your favorite color?"

"Sky blue pink," she replied. "Tag, what has gotten into you?"

He arranged his face into a leer. "It's more like what I've gotten into, and that would be you."

Her shoulders slumped, as if she'd been tense and could finally relax. Since when was Red uptight around him? She was supposed to be at ease. Happy. Secure.

Something was wrong. Not as wrong as things had been in New Orleans, but still not the way they'd been before pitchers and catchers reported for spring training. Before she'd gone to Florida with the rest of the team.

"Do you want to see if there's a spring training game on TV?"

"I don't have cable or a satellite dish," she said. "No time to watch, remember?"

That and her strict budget. She was real good at denying herself. Like denying herself him.

He reached for her hand. He'd never noticed how finely boned her fingers were. He'd watched her wield a knife, watched her beat the hell out of raw chicken with a mallet, but had never paid attention to the hand that gripped the tools.

Something so fragile shouldn't be as strong and capable as Red was.

He'd never noticed anyone's hands before. Baseball players wore batting gloves or fielding gloves. He couldn't help but smile when he thought of Red in her oven mitts.

"What?" she asked.

"Aren't you going to introduce me to your goldfish?" He'd been teasing her about having a goldfish almost since he'd met her.

"I don't want you to corrupt her," Red replied.

He couldn't tell if she was returning the grief or if she was serious.

"She's getting nice and fat, just in time for Passover, when I'll turn her into a gefilte fish. Stress will make her lose weight."

That went over his head.

"Besides, I doubt you can climb to the third floor."

"You're right." He was better than he'd been, but he was nowhere near 100 percent. And he never would be. When he'd left New Orleans, he'd left behind the most innovative physical therapy for his type of injury in the country. But Hector Michaud, genius physical therapist, had been blunt at their last session. Tag would never regain full use of his leg. He would never play another major league baseball game. His limp was never going away but would stay with him forever, like a pungent, never-ending fart.

Not that he'd shared that information with anyone, not even Bluto, his therapist in Columbia.

"The fact that I'm here, knowing full well I can't manage the stairs to your bed ought to tell you something." He practically grumbled the words. He shouldn't have had to point that out to her.

"That's why I can't figure out why you are here," she replied.

"Why can't you believe I miss you?"

Her lagoon-colored gaze leveled on him, as calm and bright as a day on the beach. "We got home yesterday. I'm trying to regroup from New Orleans."

He could understand that.

"I'm trying to forget that Drake Dixon has quite possibly destroyed any chance I ever had at being a successful caterer or anything else, for that matter. That your pal Noah Nash helped him."

"Nash was never my pal." But Red didn't seem to hear him.

"And that your girlfriend played a major part in that destruction. You can prove you weren't doping. I can't prove anything." Bitterness dripped from every word.

"Terra isn't my girlfriend. I fucked her once in a while."

"And you fucked me once in a while. And now it's over."

"Over?" The word was a physical blow. If she'd kneed him in the balls or taken a cane to his bad knee, he couldn't have been more surprised. "Since when do friendships end unless one person betrays the other?" There hadn't been a moment when he'd believed she'd sent the e-mail containing a photo of a packing slip for anabolic steroids to the press. He'd even seen the e-mail, and not once did he entertain the thought that Red was behind it.

Her wonderful, luscious lips thinned. "Unless the friendship itself becomes a betrayal."

Another body blow. He nearly staggered. "What are you talking about?"

The brightness in her eyes was the sheen of unshed tears. He saw that now. "I'm talking about this whole friends-with-benefits thing. Turns out it wasn't very beneficial to me at all."

Tag waited until ten the following morning before he called Red. After she'd skewered him, he needed to lick his wounds and come up with a plan. He'd lost so much since October. Other than his injury, Red was the only constant. The thing he needed in his life. She made him feel better about himself. So he sat at his desk in his penthouse with his second cup of coffee, reading the e-mail from his brother.

This could work.

Red still wouldn't pick up the phone when she saw his number. So he left a message: "My brothers are coming for a visit tomorrow. I'd like to hire you to cook a couple of dinners."

There. Detached. Professional. His brothers would be staying with him, so there were bound to be some rowdy times, but he wouldn't have it any other way. Maybe other people stuck their visiting family in hotels, but not Tag Gentry. Well, maybe if his sisters with their rug rats showed up, but that wasn't likely.

But his brothers? Nothing but good times. The three of them had been close once.

Red called him back several hours later. "Use another caterer."

"You're my caterer."

"I'm booked."

Ha! "I haven't even told you the date."

She sighed. "You said tomorrow."

Tag pictured her closing her eyes. Pinching the bridge of her nose as she sometimes did when she was frustrated.

"Remember how busy I was before Dixon's Halloween party? I'm that kind of busy now for the Purim Carnival."

"You're also not catering for a team playing in the World Series or cooking three meals a day for a shut-in. You can fit in two dinner parties. I know what I want, and you're the person who cooks what I want."

Silence.

"Red, come on. I need you."

"That's the problem. That's always the problem, isn't it?"

"My brothers want to meet you. I've been singing your praises to my family."

"I don't want to meet them." Her tone was sharp. Decisive.

"Why? What's wrong with my brothers? They're nice guys. Just because we grew up on a farm doesn't make them animals. Hunter...does aerospace stuff and Cooper is a plastic surgeon."

"Specializing in breast reduction and implants."

Her sarcasm was so heavily weighted he nearly dropped his phone. "How did you know that?"

Another pause. Not quite as lengthy. "You told me about them while we were in New Orleans."

"Oh." He vaguely recalled a conversation with her. He picked up his mug and sipped.

"About them and the neighbor girl. Or did you make up that whole story about the deacon's daughter and the border collie?"

Tag choked on his coffee and then laughed. "Christi Fellows? Nope. That was true. That was also a very long time ago. We've all grown up."

Christi Fellows was a neighbor girl who put out. The Gentry brothers were red-blooded males with healthy appetites. Tag had learned a lot about sex from Christi, who was generous as well as adventurous. He'd have to ask his brothers if they knew what really happened to Christi. They shared some great times together. All four of them. "So my brothers will be here Friday and Saturday. We'll need dinner for those two nights. I thought that chicken and zucchini thing you make one night—just for laughs, you know. I think we all vowed to never eat another zucchini as long as we lived."

"I'm so glad my food amuses you."

"You ever live on a farm during zucchini season?" he asked. "If you did, you'd understand. My mother cooked zucchini seven hundred ways to Sunday."

"Maybe she should have given some to Christi Fellows," Red said. "She could have used three or so when you and your brothers weren't around."

Coffee spurted out of Tag's nose. He whooped. Nobody could make him laugh the way Red could.

"So you'll do it?" he asked. He knew better than to assume anything with Red.

"Since you asked so nicely. I'll prep the meals at my place and drop them off with reheating instructions."

That was not going to work. He wanted his brothers to meet Red. Hang with her. Get to know and appreciate her.

"Why don't you cook it in my kitchen, then you won't have to worry about toting everything up the elevator."

"No, just the ingredients."

Her sarcasm put his teeth on edge.

"Look. I want you to meet my brothers, okay? I want you to...act as my hostess. You're supposed to be my friend. Can't you do this for me?"

"That's really not a good idea."

"It's just dinner."

"Maybe I have other plans. My world doesn't revolve around you and your whims."

What the hell was a whim? And since he knew Red didn't have a social life, what possible plans could she have except work? And if she was going to work, she could damn well work for him. "Compromise," he said. Offered, really. He could meet her halfway. After all, he wasn't a stalker. He simply wanted to be with her.

"Your idea of compromise," she said in a snarky tone, "is we do what you want, and I shut up about it."

Okay, now she was pissing him off. "Actually, I was going to suggest you stay for dinner only one night. Day after tomorrow. But if working for me is going to turn you into a bitch, forget I even called."

He nearly slammed down the receiver on his desk phone when she yelped, "Wait."

So he waited. Without speaking. He was steamed.

"Do you swear it's only dinner?" Her voice shook.

He wondered what else she had in mind.

"Dinner. Meet my brothers. That's it."

"And any time I want to leave, I can?"

"When have I ever held you prisoner?" He couldn't believe she'd asked such a question.

"You got cranky on me in New Orleans when I wanted to leave."

"I didn't want you to abandon me to Noah and Terra's tender mercies. I shouldn't even have to explain that to you." He'd been helpless in New Orleans. In a strange city. Without the resources he had in Columbia, where he was a hero. Not that he took advantage of his status, but it was always there at the back of his mind. Columbia was a safe zone. His safe zone.

"All right," Red said. "I'll bring your supper to you to-morrow night, and I'll cook, serve, and dine with you the night after."

"You don't need to sound so excited."

"Don't push your luck. I'll see you tomorrow."

Skye dropped her phone to the wooden counter and then buried her face in her palms. She was pathetic. All Tag had to do was quirk a little finger, and she came running like a well-trained, desperate bimbo.

Clearly her pep talks to her mirror weren't having much of an effect on her.

Meeting his visiting brothers wasn't the same thing as being taken home to meet his parents. Except Tag had told her about the sharing of the neighbor girl when they were all teenagers. The sexual sharing. Things so nasty she couldn't even imagine some of what he'd tried to explain. And he'd followed up his story with her first experience with anal sex. Which hadn't been bad. Even now, a week later, her sphincter clenched when she thought of what Tag had done to her. She had every reason to be nervous about meeting his horn-dog brothers.

Why couldn't she say no to him? If she couldn't say no when it didn't matter, like now, how well would she fare when the stakes were high?

She was still stewing fifteen minutes later when the phone rang again. If that was Tag, she...but no. *Joel Green.* As soon as she saw his name, her throat seemed to collect the rest of her internal organs and hold them hostage.

What did he want now?

"Joel Green here. From the Jewish Community Center." His tone was a lot more pleasant than it had been in person the previous day.

"Mr. Green." At least she had a voice, considering the lack of real estate around her larynx. "I wasn't expecting to hear from you again so soon."

"Call me Joel. Please. Mr. Green is my father."

"Is there something I can help you with?"

"I was wondering how preparation for the carnival food is going."

Oh-kay. That was odd.

"Everything is fine. Thanks for asking."

"No glitches?"

"Nope. All good."

An awkward silence ensued for a moment.

Then Joel sighed. "Look. I want to apologize for my...hostility when we met."

"No need to apologize." Skye heard the formal note in her voice. The right thing to say versus the truth. Except he didn't need to apologize. He was the client, even if he hadn't been the one to hire her.

"Whatever is going on between you and Tag Gentry is none of my business. You must have had your reasons for exposing his steroid use."

Her body parts had returned to their proper locations, because her throat muscles contracted in their own version of labor. "Tag Gentry doesn't use steroids, and he can prove it if he wants to." She didn't mention her involvement or lack thereof in the public outcry against steroid use in baseball.

"I would think he'd want to clear his name. And yours."

One would think. His agent's stupid idea about marriage wasn't going to prove anything, except reinforce the idea she had Tag by the privates when the real problem was his privacy. Yeah, she could reveal the extent of his injuries and expose the daily urine tests that proved he wasn't doping, but telling his secrets wasn't right. Until he came to terms with the loss of his baseball career, he was his own worst enemy. He'd rather let the world believe he was on steroids than admit the great Tag Gentry was no more. Until he came clean about that, any attempt to clear her own name would be an exercise in futility. And he might never forgive her. Maybe she didn't want to marry him, but she also didn't want him to hate her.

"Everybody has their own agenda," was the only thing Skye added to the topic. "Tag isn't part of my ability to cater your event."

"I was wondering if I could stop by your facility and take a tour."

Skye forced a laugh. One of the few things she liked about talking on the phone was the ability to hide her face and the expressions she couldn't control. Like now. "The rabbinical council already toured and approved the facilities," she said. "But if you really want to see them, sure. When would be a good time?"

"How about five minutes? I'm only a few blocks from the address listed on the contract."

Skye looked around her kitchen. Not the one Joel would be inspecting—because that was what his impromptu request boiled down to—but the main kitchen, where a stockpot bubbled on a back burner of her make-do stove. The aroma of chicken soup in progress steamed its way into every crevice of the old building. Thank goodness she wasn't making deviled eggs. She'd freeze the stock to use in the future, substituting it for oil whenever she could.

"Sure. Um, park around back. There's an alley."

"I see it," Joel said and disconnected the call.

He must have been parked on the street when he made the call. A niggle of resentment tugged at her as she tucked her phone into her jeans pocket. She didn't even have time to change her apron. The white fabric resembled the early stages of a Jackson Pollock painting, spattered with bits of orange carrot, pale green celery, and flecks of darker green dill weed. She barely had time to whip off the offending garment and stuff it in the cabinet under the sink before the knocking on the door began.

She ran her hands over her undisciplined hair before she answered the door.

She'd forgotten that Joel Green was good-looking in a magazine-model kind of way. Which so meant she wasn't attracted to him. A face that was almost gaunt, with high, sharp cheekbones and nose. Eyes as vivid blue as an icy January morning in New England. Brown hair, the natural color of which was masked by product. Too much musky cologne. A gag-worthy amount. Joel's khaki slacks had a knife-sharp crease up the center of the leg as did the long sleeves of his white and maroon striped shirt. She wondered if he ironed his own clothes or sent them out. Not that it mattered. She just hadn't met many people with intentional creases in their clothes.

"Come in," she said. She started to apologize for the mess but snapped her mouth shut. The kitchen really wasn't a mess. She'd been cooking. The room looked like the workspace it was.

His musk nearly overpowered the comforting fragrance of the stockpot.

Maybe the space was shabby, with the used stove, exposed brick walls, and cracked tile floors. But it had passed health department inspections.

"This is the main kitchen," she said. In case he couldn't figure that out. "I prep cook for the Gems here, as well as other events. Weddings and such. I have a couple of dinner parties coming up later this week." She was babbling. As much as she tried to tell herself Joel Green had no right to judge her, her honest self had to admit he did. Well, not her. But her facilities.

"I have two other kitchen areas. One is vegan. I call it Kosher for Lent." She forced her mouth into a smile. "No animal products at all. I'm very careful about using tree nuts and gluten products in that space, too."

Not a single reaction on the screen of Joel's face.

She led the way to her certified kosher food prep area. It was a completely separate room. She'd personally stayed up many a night retiling the floors and walls in white ceramic squares, which were easy to maintain. One half of the room was designated—and labeled—meat. The other half was for dairy foods. Part of *kashrut* was not mixing meat and dairy products. She'd had to invest in two sets of everything—from refrigerators to pots and pans and implements. Even her dishwasher had separate racks. By next year, she hoped to be enough ahead that she could repeat the process for Passover, which required yet another separate set of everything because nothing that had come into contact with grains could be used for Passover. Yes, it was an investment she couldn't necessarily afford, but the earning potential was good. She'd done her research before investing. And she was fascinated by the processes and the inventiveness of kosher cooks.

She stood in the door while Joel explored. She didn't have to worry about him cross contaminating the dairy forks with the meat knives.

Her cell phone buzzed against her hip. She couldn't afford to ignore it. Even if it was Tag. The kosher kitchen, her stove issue—if Tag was willing to pay her to feed his brothers, she couldn't turn down the work.

She told herself she was being practical. Her fluctuating emotions when it came to Tucker Alexander Gentry had no bearing on her accepting the job. She stepped out of the kitchen to take his call. "What? I'm with a client right now."

"Well, you have another client at your back door," he snapped back. "You need to get the doorbell fixed and an intercom system."

"People in hell need ice water too," she replied as she hurried to let him in.

Maybe seeing Tag hire her services would go a long way toward putting some of Joel's doubts to rest.

She opened the door and let Tag in.

"You ought to give me my own key," he grumbled.

"Fat chance," she muttered under her breath. "As I said, I have another client inspecting the kosher facilities, so just sit tight and try to behave."

"I'm always good," he said, his grin cocky, almost arrogant.

"Everything appears to be in order," Joel said as he walked into the kitchen. He didn't sound happy. He stopped when he saw Tag.

"Joel, this is Tag Gentry. Tag, Joel Green from the Columbia Jewish Community Center."

Neither man said anything for a long moment. Then Tag took the initiative. "You're the festival Red's catering."

"Red?"

Tag grinned. "It's my pet name for Celeste."

"Celeste?"

"My given name," Skye hastened to explain. "I prefer to be called Skye."

Tag limped closer to her. Draped an arm over her shoulder. "She's my personal caterer."

"Then you're not upset with her?"

"Why would I be upset with my best friend?"

Skye tried to squirm away from Tag's embrace, but he tightened his fingers on her biceps.

"The website article—"

"Haven't you heard? The Internet is plagued by fake news. Red and I were victims. Her phone was stolen along with the fake invoice she was planning to burn." Tag laughed, as if the whole thing was a big joke. "You should have seen her panic when she thought she'd lost all her notes for your festival."

Joel's frostbitten gaze fixed on Skye. "Why didn't you mention this when I asked you about it the other day?"

Tag tightened his fingers even more.

Skye lifted her chin. "I was hired to cater your festival. My personal life has nothing to do with my ability to provide the JCC with what they contracted for. I refuse to be distracted from my job by other people's gullibility."

Not to mention that she couldn't prove a thing. There *had* been an invoice for steroids addressed to Tag. Someone *had* taken a photo of the document and e-mailed it to a reporter from Skye's phone.

"Besides," Tag added, "she doesn't blame Terra Baldwin for being jealous and vindictive. What is it you said, sweetheart? When they go low, we go high?"

Joel shook his head. Skye tried to shake off Tag, who only pulled her closer.

"I'm afraid I don't understand," Joel said.

"There's nothing to understand." Skye snaked her arm around Tag's waist...and pinched him. Hard. Even twisted the bit of flesh between the pads of her fingers.

He flinched. Barely.

"Terra and I used to...be involved. Now we're not."

"And now you and Skye are?" Joel asked.

Tag grinned. "You catch on quick."

Joel turned to Skye. "I'm glad I had a chance to look over your facilities. Thanks for letting me in with no notice."

"I'm used to surprise inspections," Skye said. "They happen all the time. I've yet to fail one." She was proud of her business. There were no shoddy practices at Skye's the Limit.

Joel said a few more inane things before he left.

As soon as he was out the door, Skye attempted to drive an elbow into Tag's gut, He was too quick for her.

"What was that all about?" she asked as she fished her apron from its hiding place.

"He was putting the make on you."

She shook her head. "Not everyone is as horny as you." Besides, she wasn't Jewish, and she had a feeling that meant a lot to Joel. Not that she was attracted to him. At all.

"He didn't shower today."

"How do you know that?"

"It's a guy trick. Use a lot of cologne, preferably musk, to hide your stink from not showering. He smelled so bad he might not have showered for a week."

Skye couldn't argue with that. "Good to know."

"You signed that contract with the JCC months ago. Why would this guy want to inspect your facilities now? Isn't the carnival next week?"

"He's the new director," Skye explained.

"You already met with him. And he put you in a bad mood. He definitely wants to put the make on you."

"He's looking for a way to get rid of me." She hadn't wanted to confess that to Tag.

"Because of the steroid story?"

"Because I'm not Jewish."

Tag pulled her into his arms, unmindful of her filthy apron. "He wants you. Bad. He's just more of a gentleman about it than Drake Dixon. Or me."

"No one ever accused you of being a gentleman." She wiggled free. She couldn't think when he was being affectionate. She lifted the lid on her stockpot and gave the contents a stir with her favorite wooden spoon. Fragrant steam billowed from the stainless steel, cleansing the air of the lingering miasma of Joel's cologne.

Tag was behind her, slipping his arms around her waist. "Don't meet with him here alone again."

"What?" The cover clattered into place on the pot.

"I don't like the way he looks at you."

"You can't vet all my clients, Tag."

"I wasn't wrong about Drake Dixon, was I?"

No. Tag had been more right about what Dixon really wanted from her than anyone had ever been correct about anything in the history of the world.

But Skye's own instincts had been unsettled around Dixon. She wasn't getting the same sort of creepy feeling from Joel Green.

"I don't want to vet all of them. Just him. And any other solitary male who comes sniffing around."

WHY COULDN'T RED ADMIT when she was wrong? Tag was worried about her. Or maybe just worried about losing her. Ever since New Orleans, she'd been trying to keep distance between them. Maybe even before that. After all, she'd merrily gone off to spring training when the pitchers and catchers reported.

He'd resorted to using his brothers' pending visit as an excuse to see her. To touch her.

Skye worked herself free of him again. "So why are you here?"

"To go over the menus for my dinner parties."

"I thought they were family meals."

Tag shrugged. "Whatever. Okay, we talked about that chicken and zucchini thing you do. Where you beat the hell out of the chicken with a hammer. Have I ever told you how sexy you are when you do that?"

Red rolled her eyes.

"I want beef the second night. Maybe that tenderloin thing you do."

"Have a seat at the island," she said, her tone weary. She pulled out her cell phone and tapped it a few times. "Okay. Let's discuss your menus."

He didn't want to talk about menus or food or even his brothers. He wanted her to acknowledge him as an important part of her life. At this point, he'd temporarily settle for being even a minor part. He didn't understand where the cold shoulder was coming from, but thinking about it kept him up at night. Up as in awake. Merely thinking about Red kept him up in other ways. That hadn't changed.

And yeah. He was jealous of Joel Green. The man was too handsome in a wimpy way, and women tended to like that look. Otherwise, male models wouldn't look exactly like him.

Tag didn't want to talk about food. He wanted to talk about what Hector had told him that final morning in New Orleans. *As radical as my therapy is, I don't think I can help you.*

Who else did he have to talk to except Red, who knew the true extent of his injuries? HIPAA laws had kept that information from the press. Only Red understood the depth of his concern.

As far as the rest of the world was concerned, all he'd suffered in that home plate collision was a compound tibial fracture. What the rookie's spikes had really accomplished was one of the best-kept secrets in the world.

Terra Baldwin had been looking for that information in New Orleans. She'd had to settle for the phony steroid story when he and Red, working together, had thwarted her quest for more information about his injuries. For all he knew, Terra had been the one to fake the story, set up by Drake Dixon and his flunky Noah Nash. Dixon got his wish. A lot of people thought Tag was a doper and that his trusted pal Celeste Schuyler had betrayed that fact to the world.

Already Red was suffering the consequences. Otherwise, that Joel Green character wouldn't have been at Skye's the Limit, sniffing around. Except she was sexy. And part of her sexiness was because she didn't know how beautiful she was. She was a cook. That's all she cared about. Including Tag. But he was going to change that.

When his agent had suggested a fake engagement to show the world a united front—that Tag knew Red hadn't betrayed him—Red was the one who balked. Tag would have happily gotten engaged to her for real, and it kind of hurt that she hadn't been nearly as enthusiastic about the idea as she should have been.

"You want something to drink?" she asked. "I have bottled water, herbal tea, and green tea."

"Water would be good. Or a beer." Or bourbon. If he wasn't going to play ball again, what was the point of trying to stay healthy?

Maybe he ought to try steroids.

"You know, marrying me would go a long way toward clearing your name."

"Or making you look whipped." She handed him a water bottle. "Or making people wonder what else you're trying to hide. You know. Like your injury is worse than you've let on, and I know it. So you married me to guarantee my silence."

He thought about it as he unscrewed the cap. "I don't think so. People believe you've already done your worst." And no one would believe his career was over. He was Tag Gentry. A baseball hero. Invincible. The leg thing—just a setback.

"Look, I appreciate your concern. And your support. But what can I do? Terra and Noah framed me solid. There *was* a packing slip for steroids addressed to you. It *was* photographed by and sent to Terra from my phone. Those are facts. Everything else is...conjecture. Or whining."

"You have no motive."

Red shrugged. "I'm broke. Maybe Terra paid me. Or maybe you spurned me, so exposing you was my revenge. Because you wouldn't pay me to keep my mouth shut."

"You're the one spurning *me*, babe." He laughed, hiding the burn of annoyance her rejection sparked.

"I have an idea." Her eyes gleamed. "Why don't I spill about your daily urine tests to another reporter? Mention that I knew about them. That I knew they were clean. Then, instead of having to marry me, you could just release the results of those tests."

"No." The denial came out more forcefully than he'd intended. He didn't want her telling anything to anyone. For several reasons. First off, he did want to marry her. Okay, tied for first—if he revealed even a little bit more about his injury, what were the chances the world would find out he was washed up as a player? He wasn't ready to admit that. Even to himself. Most of the time. If he wasn't a ballplayer, who was he?

He slammed his bottle onto the counter so hard water sloshed over his hands. "I trust you not to say anything about the pee tests."

She turned away from him. Opened her refrigerator and stood in front of it, her back to him. "Of course. What else do I have to lose?"

FRIDAY, MARCH 3

Skye started shopping for Tag's first dinner party almost immediately. He had a great refrigerator at his place. He had a fabulous kitchen, period. She'd used it during the World Series when her stove died. There was no reason she couldn't purchase the food while she had a little breathing space and then store it at his penthouse.

She still had her key to his place. Maybe she should have returned it to him once he was no longer wheelchair-bound, but she'd spent a lot of time with him, even after her contract to feed him ran out. Faking friendship. Pretending the relationship was only about sex. Denying her growing feelings for him.

First up, his request for chicken and zucchini. Very easy to prepare in small batches. Tag had told her there would be only the three of them for dinner the first night of his brothers' visit.

Zucchini in March was not inexpensive or particularly appealing visually, but she wasn't serving it raw. She shifted the bag in her hand and strode across the lobby to the elevator that would take her to Tag's penthouse. Just as the doors were about to slide shut, a man pushed a small black suitcase between the panels and then joined her in the car.

She'd never seen him before, but by his dark hair and the gray eyes that examined her so minutely, she guessed he was one of Tag's brothers. Had to be. His gaze was almost familiar, but in a creepy way. Besides, who else would be on the elevator to the penthouse? Well, it wasn't her place to say anything. She was only the caterer. She stepped closer to the control panel. Just in case the man wasn't related to Tag. Because he was staring at her far too intently for comfort. This wasn't simply the normal *I'm-stuck-on-an-elevator-with-a-strange man* paranoia most aware women felt. Every hair on her body stood on end.

When the elevator stopped at Tag's floor, Skye got off without looking back.

"My brother must be holding out on us." The brother spoke in a deep, richly timbred voice.

"I doubt it," Skye replied. "I'm just the hired help."

The door to the penthouse swung open as she was about to insert her key.

"Red." Tag sounded pleased to see her. He scooped her into an embrace. "I didn't realize you were coming around so early. And I see you've met Hunter."

No wonder she'd felt like trapped prey in the elevator.

"We haven't introduced ourselves," the brother said. "Red?"

"Celeste Schuyler," Tag replied. "My older brother, Hunter Gentry."

Skye squirmed out of Tag's embrace. "Nice to meet you," she lied and then headed for the kitchen. She had work to do.

Okay, maybe she was predisposed to think poorly of Tag's brothers after the story he'd told her about the foursome with the neighbor girl. But Tag had been part of that, and she didn't think any less of him because he'd done it. So that made her guilty of double standard, which she hated. She wanted to be fair. And the guy wasn't responsible for his aggressive name. That had been his parents' doing.

"Wait a minute." The brother's tone was sharp enough to cut glass. "Celeste Schuyler? Isn't that the woman who sent the anabolic steroid information to that reporter?"

Skye kept her back to the men and her spine stiff as she walked toward the kitchen.

"Her name was on the e-mail," she heard Tag say. "But she didn't send it."

That damned e-mail was going to haunt her for the rest of her life. At least Tag hadn't, even for a millisecond, believed she'd been the one to tell a reporter he was doping.

Sometimes that steadfast faith in her was all that kept her going. But steadfast faith wasn't deep. She was still only a booty call. A former booty call. No more. Her heart couldn't take it.

The kitchen was just as empty and echoing as it had been the first time she'd seen it. Stainless steel professional grade appliances. Marble countertops. No magnets on the fridge. Nothing personal or homey in sight.

But that was just Tag. He abhorred clutter. Messes of any kind. Including relationship messes.

Well, she wasn't going to mess up his life any more than she already had.

She'd started cutting boneless, skinless breasts of chicken into bite-sized pieces when Tag joined her.

"Where's your brother?" she asked, hoping Hunter wouldn't follow.

"Unpacking," Tag replied. "I've already warned him you're hands off. He had the same look in his eye that Joe Green had."

"Joel. Thanks. I'm glad I didn't have to try to explain about bad vibes."

"He's a little aggressive. Always has been."

"Is he a football or rugby player?" Tag's knives weren't nearly as sharp as her own were, so the blade didn't slice easily through the chicken flesh.

"Believe it or not, he's an aerospace engineer."

She put down the knife. "You're kidding." Aerospace engineers were nerds. No way was Hunter Gentry a nerd.

"I know. Looks and brains. The rest of the family got shortchanged. Greedy bastard." Tag's tone was easy, as if he were relating something not important.

"He's the oldest?" Skye asked.

"Hunter, Harper, me, Piper, and Cooper."

That large a family boggled Skye's mind. Most of her childhood had been spent with her wandering salesman father, after her mother had died when she was eight. Her father had passed when Skye was eighteen, but it felt as if she'd been on her own her entire life.

"Maybe all that time in the lab and figuring equations stunted his social skills." As long as Tag kept him away from her, she could afford to be...open-minded.

"He really scared you." Tag sounded surprised.

"I'm still on edge from New Orleans." New Orleans could be blamed for a lot of things.

"Hey." Tag covered one of her hands with his. "You're safe here. You're safe from my brother. He was just being a jerk, trying to get a rise out of me. You know how it is."

"Nope. Don't have brothers or sisters. My understanding of family dynamics comes from reruns of *The Brady Bunch*."

Tag laughed. "What about your goldfish? Or isn't he allowed to watch TV?"

"She's too busy gaining weight to watch TV." Skye resumed her cutting. For some reason, the odor of the raw chicken was getting to her. "I'm sorry. Maybe I'm overreacting to your brother."

"Don't apologize. His social skills are geeky too. "

"Are you saying you got all the charm in the family?" Skye forced her mouth into a smile. This was what she missed about being with Tag. The lighthearted banter. The playful dissing of each other.

"If you want to call it charm. I'm one of those middle children who would do anything for attention. "

"Anything?"

"Almost."

"How about slicing a zucchini?" Skye asked.

"Hey. That's why I'm paying you the big bucks."

"I suppose that means you won't dice the tomatoes for me either."

"I always said you were one smart cookie, Cookie."

"You should go find your brother and make sure he steers clear of the kitchen while I fix your dinner," Skye said. The chicken was cut. She washed the knife in steaming water and soap. This was the only knife Tag owned that was anywhere close to being decent. She knew she should have brought her own. Or prepped everything in her kitchen and brought it here to assemble and cook.

But she couldn't stay away from Tag. Pathetic. Looking for any excuse to spend time with him. Maybe he'd come to her about cooking for his brothers, but she should have stuck to her guns when she said no.

Slicing the squash, chopping the onion, and dicing the tomatoes went fairly smoothly. Cooking such a small amount of food was something she could do with her eyes closed. Once everything was assembled, she texted the final heating instructions to Tag. He could handle the microwave.

Skye rode the elevator to the ground floor in solitude and then crossed the building lobby, her soft-soled clogs soundless on the glistening marble floor. She pushed on the heavy glass door, vaguely wondering why there was a crowd on the sidewalk.

"Skye!"

She looked toward the caller and realized whoever it was had a camera. Aimed at her.

The press.

"Over here, Skye!"

She put her head down and tried to strong-arm her way through the melee to her van, which was parked on the next block. What was this all about?

"Are you trying to beg Tag's forgiveness?" someone else shouted.

The words were like a body blow. Of course the press knew where Tag lived. And someone had probably seen her van with its *Skye's the Limit* logo on the side, put two and two together and come up with something so far from the truth it would be believed in these alt-fact days.

Someone grabbed her arm. Firmly.

"Let go unless you want a lawsuit," she snarled.

"Oh, I don't think so."

She looked up into familiar stormy gray eyes in yet another strange face.

"You must be Cooper. Your brothers are upstairs waiting for you."

If he was surprised she knew his name, he didn't show it.

He pulled her back toward Tag's building, far more effective against the herd of reporters than she was.

"Let go of me."

"Not on your life."

She could try to make a scene, but everyone believed she'd done Tag wrong, so she doubted anyone would come to her aid.

She knew what Cooper—he didn't deny his identity—was doing. She said nothing as she allowed him to lead her through the lobby. To the elevator. To the penthouse.

Tag opened the door. "Coop! Red?"

"I found her skulking around outside your building," Cooper said as he dragged her into the entry.

"Skulking?"

"I parked my van down the block," Skye replied. "There are a lot of reporters out there. I guess the van tipped them off that I was here."

"I should hope so." Cooper still sounded furious.

Just to mess with him, Skye slid past him, snuggled against Tag, tiptoed to brush her lips against his. "Enjoy dinner." She made her voice as sexy as she could. Which probably wasn't very. "See you tomorrow."

Tag's eyes widened before he hauled her against his body and slipped his tongue into her mouth. "Are you sure you can't stay tonight?" he asked, once he let her go.

"No. You need some time alone to catch up with your brothers." She turned to their audience. "Bye, Cooper. Nice meeting you."

"WHAT THE HELL was that about?"

Tag wanted to laugh in Coop's face. Coop had always been an arrogant little shit. All was well in the world.

"Red does my catering," Tag explained.

"She accused you of using steroids. Publicly."

"No she didn't."

"I saw her name on the e-mail that *Sportsworld Insider* put on their website," Coop insisted.

"Long, boring story," Tag replied. "Red and I are getting married."

Coop narrowed his eyes. "Married?"

"Yes. If Red wants a big fancy to-do, will you be one of my ushers?"

"Not the best man? Oh. Wait. That's Hunter's honor, isn't it."

"I wouldn't worry. Red's not the type to fuss. We'll probably elope."

"When is the happy day?" Coop slid off his expensive overcoat and handed it to Tag. "And do the folks know?"

"I have to get her to agree, first," Tag admitted as he opened the closet door.

"Really? I would have thought she'd be hard-pressed to get *you* to agree. I take it Hunter is already here."

"In the living room." Tag stopped looking for an empty hanger and waved in the general direction of Hunter's whereabouts.

"What's his take on your impending nuptials?"

"Haven't told him yet. But he likes Red. Maybe too much." He hung the coat over one of his own.

"Made a play for her, did he?"

"I set him straight without violence."

Tag led the way to where he'd left his older brother. He'd seen them both at Christmas, when they'd all managed to get to their parents' for the holiday. He wasn't sure why they'd decided to converge on him now.

He let Hunter fix Coop something to drink. His leg seemed to be going through withdrawal after being manipulated by Hector in New Orleans. Not even Bluto's ministrations that morning eased the pain. Tag eased into his recliner. Declined the drink Hunter offered him. Closed his eyes.

"Are we boring you?" Coop asked.

"No. It's been a long day." Long...and wearisome. He should be in Florida with the rest of the Columbia Gems. Pre-season games. His brain and most of his body were set like an alarm clock.

"So how are those steroids working for you?" Coop asked.

"What steroids?" Tag kept his eyes shut. Coop could be obnoxious, and this conversation was beginning to have the makings of massive tedium.

"Come on. You think we don't read all the news about you? The dumb jock gets all the glory in this family."

"Yawn," Tag said. "You're such a smart guy, you ought to know better than to believe everything you read. And you're a titty doctor. You ought to know women a little better. Or are they only boobs to you?"

Hunter snorted.

"What's that supposed to mean?" Coop sounded cranky.

Good.

"Terra Baldwin broke the alleged story. Apparently I broke her heart when I stopped crawling between her legs." Tag opened his eyes. Smiled at his brothers. "Terra was with me in New Orleans. Along with Red."

"Who's Red?" Coop asked.

"Celeste Schuyler, the owner of Skye's the Limit. You know, the woman you accosted on the street and dragged up here a few minutes ago."

"I'm confused," Coop said.

"You're an ass," Tag replied.

Hunter chimed in. "I think I get it. You were in New Orleans with the caterer, whom you're involved with, and the reporter didn't like the attention you weren't giving her, so she set up something to make it look like the caterer was accusing you of using steroids."

Thank goodness someone in the family was smart.

"That's about it," Tag replied. "Revenge as a two-pronged tongue."

"I don't suppose you can prove otherwise."

Tag stretched. The muscles in his arms and shoulders appreciated the movement. "I peed in a cup every time I saw the physical therapist in New Orleans. And let me tell you, that guy would have inverted my ass if anything illegal or even some legal shit had shown up."

"So why aren't you telling this to the world to clear up your reputation?" Coop asked.

"I have my reasons." That he wasn't about to share with the Geek and the Doc.

Coop and Hunter might be his brothers, but that didn't mean they had to know just how scared he was about his leg. Especially them. The brothers were the Geek, the Jock, and the Doc. Those successful Gentry brothers, fresh off the farm. They were the pride of their tiny, rural school district. Hibbing High in Minnesota touted Bob Dylan's Nobel Prize in Literature. Consolidated Central in Sloatesville, Georgia, had their own bragging rights.

He was part of that. He could not fail.

Nor could he afford anyone finding out about the extent of the injury inflicted by an overzealous rookie sliding into home plate in the top of the ninth inning of Game Seven of the National League Championship Series. Kind of hard to hide a compound tibial fracture on national TV, but the rest of the mangling from the kid's cleats? No one except the doctors, the physical therapists, team management, and Red knew about that. And maybe not even Red. He hadn't told her. But she knew things about him from deep in her soul.

If he told the world about his daily urine tests, the full story of his treatment with Hector Michaud might come out. Hector had a reputation among professional athletes for taking on only the most hard-core cases. Bad enough that reporter in New Orleans had tried to interview the guy. Fortunately, the local news story hadn't been picked up by any of the syndicated services, so not many people knew Tag had been doing PT with Hector. Because once that news got out... He wasn't ready for that. He wasn't ready to admit he would never recover enough to return to the diamond.

Besides, there was collateral damage. In this case, Red would suffer even more than she already was stigmatized. Bad enough the world already believed she'd betrayed him by announcing his alleged steroid use. If people believed she'd made up the whole story— She was right. Terra and Noah had done a good job of framing her. Framing her? Destroying her.

If only there were a way to make Terra confess her complicity.

He looked Coop in the eye. "Let's just say my reasons are valid and leave it at that."

"Pretty impressive fake e-mail," Hunter said.

"It wasn't faked in the way you're thinking. Someone stole Red's phone and used it to scan the packing slip for the steroids, then send the whole thing to Terra."

"Who would do something that convoluted?" Hunter asked.

"Terra," Tag replied. "She's a devious bitch, completely without morals or integrity."

"Do you know for a fact Terra stole Red's phone?"

"I was there when Red discovered her phone was missing. I was there when Red discovered the phone in Terra's pocket, and heard Terra tell Red she'd found the phone on the front steps of the house we were all staying in."

"Sounds like a lot of trouble to me," Hunter mumbled.

"Terra is desperate. She's made a couple of bad career decisions and is trying to get back on the fast track. She thought because I used to fuck her, she could get the dirty on me."

"That's just wrong. So how does she fit into your life now? Does Red or whatever her name is have a problem with her?"

"Terra isn't part of my life. Red is. And I'm going to do anything I can to protect her. Now let's change the subject."

Until he got things settled with her, he didn't want his family peering too closely into their relationship.

SATURDAY, MARCH 4

Skye let herself into Tag's penthouse, wheeling a crate of ingredients behind her. She'd kept things simple for his first dinner with his family. Now it was time to knock their socks off.

Although why she cared what his brothers thought about her cooking, she couldn't say. She gotten up early that morning and made onion jam in her main kitchen while she baked hamantaschen—the three-cornered filled cookies named after the hat of the villain of the Purim story—in her kosher kitchen. She made sure there were plenty of apricot-filled ones for Joel Green's sweet tooth.

Grilled chicken breasts with onion balsamic jam and a steamed vegetable medley, full of colors, textures, and flavors. Healthy, but elegant. Sure, Tag wanted beef, but that was just his wounded ego talking. Her farewell dinner for him wasn't going to be one that would kill him.

Because this absolutely had to be the last contact they had. She was helping him out as a friend. That was all.

Only her phone disturbed her as she prepped the vegetables in Tag's kitchen, which was almost as familiar to her as her own. Another cancellation. Bridal shower this time. Columbia's Great Gardeners had already cancelled her services for their soiree mid-April. They'd just made their thirty-day deadline.

Her cancellation policy was probably the only reason she still had the Purim Carnival job. Any other kosher caterer was likely already booked, so the JCC had no option but to honor their contract with her.

The glob of bitterness in her throat didn't want to dissolve. Things weren't going well at all. Ever since Mardi Gras. Since Terra Baldwin's sabotage, business had fallen off. Jobs she'd bid on that she thought she'd win weren't coming through. A slew of cancellations. And the silence from the Gems baseball organization.

That one really bothered her. Tag had blackmailed majority shareholder Drake Dixon into promising a renewal on Skye's contract with the team. She'd been asked to go to spring training. Which she had. Okay, Drake Dixon had been charged with illegal gambling, but her contract should have been in the works. Every time she called the front office, she got a run-around.

Her gut told her Dixon hadn't done a thing to expedite her contract, and now it was moot. The team would never hire her now, not after what Terra had done with the fake e-mail.

She sliced the blade of her knife through the red pepper and into the wood of her cutting board.

Seemed like every time she used Tag's kitchen, she was stressing about money.

"If I hadn't smelled the food, I wouldn't have known you were here," Tag said from the doorway.

Skye forced a smile. "Good. I still have my key, which I will return as soon as I'm finished with the vegetables."

"You don't need to return it." His black brows rushed together, and he sounded irritated. "You're going to need it after we're married."

"Don't start," she said in a low voice. "Let's just get through tonight in a civil manner. I will play your loving fiancée in public for your brothers, but after tonight, I think we need to cool it a while."

The spot in his cheek usually reserved for a dimple twitched. "What if I don't want to?"

"We've been doing our relationship—if you want to call it that—your way since the beginning. Isn't it my turn?" Yeah, she owed him for rescuing her from Drake Dixon's assault back in October. But Dixon was in enough trouble now that he shouldn't be bothering Skye anymore.

Except by not renewing her contract with the Gems. His ultimate revenge.

"Actually, we've been running our relationship according to your agenda," Tag said. "If I had my way, you'd be in my bed every night."

"That's not how friends with benefits work."

"How would you know? I don't think you've benefited very many other men with your friendship."

Skye's cheeks heated. "You're right. You would know more about casual sex than I would."

"Damn right I do. And I've never made a secret of it or pretended otherwise." He crossed his arms over his chest and leaned against the doorjamb. "And I've never asked another woman to marry me either."

"You didn't ask me. Your agent did. You know, the marriage-of-convenience storyline in a book or movie is not one of my favorites. Real life doesn't make it any more palatable."

Tag at least had the courtesy to wince. "I can't exactly get down on one knee," he reminded her.

He had offered to take her shopping for a ring. But that, at least the way he'd phrased it, was more of a public relations move than a romantic gesture. No, Skye didn't expected roses, champagne, poetry, or any other stereotypical romantic trope. She didn't even really want them. But she did want sincerity. Love. Commitment, not convenience.

She loved him so much. Giving him up was going to be the hardest thing she'd ever done in her life.

TAG WATCHED RED mutilate deserving vegetables. Except the mushrooms. She shouldn't have been so violent with them. Something that thrived on shit and darkness shouldn't be so desecrated. She was vicious with that knife of hers. Since he was clearly annoying her, he thought it best to keep his distance.

What he couldn't figure out was why there had to be distance at all. He'd proposed to her. He thought that meant maybe they'd be spending more time together. Nope. She might as well have been in Florida with the team again for all the togetherness that transpired. If he hadn't sought her out to cater meals for his visiting brothers, he might not even be seeing her now.

Her phone rang. She wiped her hands on her white apron before checking to see who might be calling.

Tag didn't want her taking other calls when she was on his clock. His time. All of her attention should be on him.

"Hi, Joel," she said, her tone a hell of a lot more chipper than it had been while she'd conversed with him. He squelched the urge to mock her. "What's up?"

Green had better not be saying what Tag was thinking.

Red scowled at him before turning away.

Damn it, she was standing in his kitchen. She had no business giving him her back.

"What kind of problem?"

Tag knew exactly what kind of problem Green had—the hots for the caterer. She, however, was taken. Tag figured he was going to have to buy her an engagement ring on his own. Surprise her with it. Maybe that was why she was so cranky. He not only hadn't dated her, he'd been matter-of-fact about getting married. Maybe she needed to be wooed. Convinced of his sincerity.

Not that he was sure how to do that. She wasn't the kind of woman to be swayed by flowers or any of the other props of courtship. Maybe he could buy her a gift card to one of the on-line book vendors so she could download more of her romance novels to read on her phone. While she was too pragmatic to expect fairy tales in real life, she did like her books. Which meant she could be swayed. He just needed to figure out how.

Because he needed her in his life the same way he need oxygen.

He didn't want to ask his brothers for advice. They had history. Knew too much about one another's past habits with women. Red deserved something more than *fuck her*. Besides. He'd tried fucking her, but she was still too aloof.

"I'm with another client right now," Red said. "And I have an event tonight, so I can't meet with you until tomorrow. Besides, isn't today your Sabbath?"

At least she wasn't blowing off dinner with him. Maybe there was some way he could take advantage of that.

"Oh. Right. It's after sundown. How about tomorrow, then. Nine o'clock at your office?"

She'd remembered her New Orleans cab driver's Sabbath just fine. This sounded to Tag as if she was flirting with Green. His mood darkened.

"Okay, I'll see you then." She disconnected the call. "Sorry about that," she said to Tag, not sounding at all sorry. "Business."

Or not. Maybe she'd wanted him to know that her dealings with Green really were strictly business.

Tag took some comfort in that thought.

"This Purim thing is a big deal. He's really stressed. It's his first big event at the center since he was hired, and he essentially inherited a plan that isn't his."

Red made it all sound so reasonable. Made Tag feel smaller than the fleck of purple onion clinging to the front of her apron.

"I know you're running a business. I hired you, remember?" Being reasonable was a struggle, but he'd do it if it killed him.

"What time do you want me to serve tonight?"

"I thought we would all have drinks together, some appetizers—I told you appetizers, didn't I?"

From the way her lips compressed, he guessed he'd probably forgotten that part.

"Crackers and cheese will be fine," he hastened to add. He knew how much effort she put into what she did. How she planned every detail. How she shopped in advance, vying for the freshest ingredients she could find.

"White flour crackers and processed cheese spread are not an option." Her voice sounded tight. She knew his habits too well.

He needed her to improve his quality of life. Not just in bed, but his diet. His happiness.

"You know, I figured you might pull a stunt like this. I'm prepared. But it will cost you extra, because I didn't stint on the cheeses."

"Of course you didn't, and nor would I want you to."

He pushed off the doorjamb. Stood close enough to smell the shampoo she'd used that morning. "I depend on you to keep me on the straight and narrow." He nuzzled her ear.

"You're an adult. How about some individual responsibility?"

He traced the coil of her ear with his tongue. "Are you getting hot? Because I take that responsibility very seriously. And believe me, it's quite adult."

"Not now. I'm working. How would you like it if I came up to you in the batting cage and did the same thing?"

He stepped back as if she'd thrown icy water on him. What if he never saw the inside of a batting cage again?

"This looks cozy."

Saved by Coop. Tag had never been so glad to see his younger brother.

"Mind if I join you?"

Red stiffened, and Tag regretted ever having told her about the neighbor girl who'd relieved the Gentry brothers of their virginities.

"What's up?" Tag asked.

"I wanted to let you know I'm going to run out for a bit—meeting someone for a cup of coffee, but I'll be back before eight. Does that work?"

Tag looked to Red, who nodded.

Tag didn't like the way Coop was eyeing Red. But she was safe. Coop was definitely a breast man and Red wasn't overly endowed in that area, even though Tag thought she was perfectly shaped.

"I'll see you later, then. Don't get started without me."

Skye wasn't exactly sure how she was supposed to handle being a guest and the caterer. Timing was everything when it came to dinner. She figured she'd skip the appetizer part of the menu while she grilled the chicken breasts.

She prepped her appetizer plates—three cheeses, grapes, whole-wheat crackers, a few almonds, and a sprig or two of basil—and set them out in Tag's living room.

She envied him the grill on his stove. A man who didn't know a stove from a campfire shouldn't be allowed to own such a fine piece of equipment. His stove was nicer than the one she'd ended up buying. The bank hadn't approved a loan for the stove of her dreams. And she'd needed a second, smaller range for her kosher kitchen. Her main stove was adequate. But nothing like Tag's. He had the best of everything. He deserved the best of everything. Except her.

She stayed busy in kitchen, not wanting to mingle with Tag's brothers until she had to. And that was the way it should be.

Tag and Hunter sipped their soft drinks in companionable silence. Coop still hadn't made it back from his meeting. Tag wasn't in the mood for alcohol. He didn't need booze to bond with his older brother, and he certainly needed all his wits to deal with Red. Who, as usual, was being contrary.

"Something smells good," Hunter finally said.

"Red is a professional. Best damn cook in South Carolina."

"You've got it bad." Hunter sipped at his cola.

"Got what bad?"

Hunter snorted. "Red fever."

Tag froze, his root beer halfway to his mouth. "Huh?"

"Have you fucked her yet? You know, to get her out of your system?"

Every ounce of Tag's self-control went into keeping from punching Hunter's mouth so hard he'd fly out the window behind him and splatter on the sidewalk fifteen stories below.

Maybe he'd just punch him gently. "Shut your filthy fucking mouth."

"I rest my case." Hunter's words were softly spoken.

"You don't know shit."

"Don't I?" Hunter smirked.

Yeah, that mouth needed to be bloodied. Tag put down his glass. Wadded his fingers into a fist.

Hunter echoed the motions. "You want to take me on? No problem. You win, I shut up. I win, I fuck your cook. And if Coop wants, he can too."

Tag charged. Ignored the agony bellowing in his leg.

His unexpected burst of speed must have surprised Hunter, because he didn't move fast enough. Tags knuckles met Hunter's face with a satisfying jar that vibrated up Tag's arm.

Hunter's head snapped back, but he held his ground. "I don't fight cripples." Blood dribbled from the side of his mouth.

"And I don't fight geeks," Tag snarled. "Except when they're assholes."

"Guys, we have company." Coop grabbed Tag's arm before he could take another swing at Hunter.

Hunter dabbed his mouth with a napkin from the pile Red had put next to the cheese plate. "Are you going to introduce us to your guest?"

Tag smelled her perfume before he turned. Wanted to take a swing at Coop too. "What the fuck is Terra Baldwin doing in my house?"

He couldn't believe his brother brought that viper bitch to a family dinner.

"Your charming brother invited me." Terra never blinked as she explained her presence. Never twitched in embarrassment or anything else. As if she had every right to invade Tag's world.

"Terra?" Hunter echoed.

"She saw me with Skye yesterday and tracked me down," Coop said. "We met for coffee, and she wheedled an invitation to dinner out of me. Maybe we could all go out."

"Go out." Tag pointed at the door. "With my blessing."

And of course that was the moment Red chose to join them. "What was all that yelling about?"

She paused in the door. Her eyes widened when she saw Terra. "Hello, Terra."

"Hi, Skye. Nice to see you again."

"Is it? What's Dixon paying you to do to me now?"

Terra laughed.

Tag seemed to be the only one who knew it was phony.

"I have no idea what you're talking about. I'm in town working on a story about pig farms. I never knew there were so many so close to Columbia." Terra shuddered ever so slightly. "You look well, Skye."

And she did. She'd taken off her inevitable white apron. She wore nice-looking blue slacks and a shiny Gems teal-and-blue-striped top. Her wild curls were piled atop her head. She'd dressed up for his family. Tag appreciated that.

"Did you cater the meal Cooper invited me to?" Terra asked. Her dark hair was smooth. Unruffled. Unnatural. Eyes the same color as bruises stared guilelessly at Red.

Tag's dick shriveled.

"Yes. Not all of my clients have deserted me because of your lies."

"You're not invited," Tag said. "If Coop invited you, I'm uninviting you. He can take you out to eat and rent a hotel room if he's so anxious to get into your pants."

Red was slinking toward the kitchen, probably hoping he wouldn't notice. Not going to work. His senses were always on high alert when it came to her. He quickly crossed to her side. Rested a restraining palm on her upper arm.

His touch alone stopped her flight. Her skin rippled beneath the fabric of her shirt. Even his calluses detected the tremor.

"Stay." He pitched his voice low enough so that only she could hear.

"I thought you might want to hear Ms. Baldwin's side of the story you told us about that e-mail," Coop said.

"I've known Terra for a couple of years. Her lies all sound the same to me."

Terra didn't even flinch. "Oh, Tag. You know it's not like that."

"Yeah, I do. Please leave. This is the last time I'm asking you nicely." He made sure his tone wasn't at all civil.

"What has that woman done to you?" Terra asked, glaring at Red.

"Fed me. Taken care of me while you were off chasing shadows in the name of a career that doesn't really exist. Taken care of me, period. The real issue is what *you* have done to me. Tried to ruin my reputation by putting lies about steroid use out on the Internet."

"I'm a reporter. What did you think I was going to do when your current bimbo e-mailed that scoop?"

Red stiffened. "Except my phone was in your pocket. Or maybe that detail slipped your mind."

"I told you. I found that phone on the sidewalk."

"Yeah. In my pocket when I was standing on the sidewalk at the Krewe D'Etat parade. How do you sleep at night?"

"Oh, please."

"You're a lying bitch," Tag said. "Coop, I'm not kidding. Get her out of here before I call the cops to report a trespasser. I don't want a conniving lying reporter in my home, and I really don't want one at my table. Have I made myself clear? Get. Her. Out."

Tag tightened his hand on Red's arm and escorted her from the room.

"I could always put a purgative in her food," Red said in a shaky voice. "You know, something to cause a digestive upset."

"You can do that?"

"I can do all kinds of things. Herbs aren't just for flavoring." She plucked her apron from a stool and put it on. "Let me check on dinner." She opened the oven door. The heat cavorted in the loose strands of hair around her face, sending the fine curls into a frenzied dance.

Tag could watch her work all day.

"I wish we were alone," he said. "I'd drag you off to bed."

Red straightened. Smiled. But it was a sad, weary smile. There was no joy. No happiness. "I don't want to be your friend with benefits anymore."

Of course, that was when Hunter decided he needed to tell them that Coop was escorting Terra down to the lobby and procuring a cab for her, so he might be late for supper.

"Look. If this is about Terra, I had no idea Coop was dragging her up here, like he dragged you up here yesterday."

"Am I interrupting something?" Hunter asked.

"Yes," Tag snapped at the same time Red said, "No."

Red pulled a pan from the oven. Scooped the contents onto a platter he was certain he'd never seen before. Picked up a dark bottle from the counter and drizzled brown liquid over the food. The sweet tang of balsamic—he'd learned the aroma from hanging around with her—melded with the savory scent of roasted vegetables.

"Don't do this," Tag said in a low voice.

"The need for the pretense has passed," Red replied at the same volume. "And it didn't work."

"Because we never announced our engagement. We never did anything with it except argue about it!" Enough with trying to be civilized. He wasn't used to being thwarted. In the end, even the most stubborn pitcher bowed to his superior knowledge.

"I'm putting dinner on the table now."

She spoke as if he'd said nothing.

"Hunter, can you get the door for me?"

His able-bodied brother rushed to comply.

Her biceps flexed under the silky material of her blouse as she picked up the vegetable-laden platter. As regal as if she were bearing crown jewels on a velvet pillow, Red carried the platter to the dining room.

Four places had been set at the table. She'd used dishes that matched the platter, which again, he could swear he'd never laid eyes on. These were white. His were brown.

"Smells great," Hunter said, as if trying to diffuse the tension.

"Thank you. If Cooper isn't back in the next ten minutes, he can heat a plate in the microwave. I'd suggest forty seconds."

"Where are you going?"

"Home." She untied her apron. Pulled it over her head. "Just rinse the dishes and toss them in the dishwasher. You'll be fine."

MAYBE TAG WOULD be fine, but if Skye didn't get out of there, and fast, she was going to lose it in a large, noisy, messy way that would only humiliate her, embarrass Hunter, and disgust Tag. Then she might never be fine again. If she fled now, there was a chance she could survive. Maybe even intact. If not...

"Are you just going to let her walk out?" she heard Hunter ask as she headed toward the kitchen.

"What do you suggest I do? Toss her over my shoulder and take her to bed? Because if that's what you're thinking, no wonder you're still single. I don't manhandle women."

As if he hadn't threatened to do just that if he weren't hampered by his lame leg.

There wasn't any point in staying. No reason for her to get to know Tag's brothers. Her choice.

She gathered the knives and other utensils she'd brought with her, as well as her bottle of balsamic vinegar and other seasonings. She didn't want to have to make a second trip to retrieve a forgotten item. No built-in excuses.

She left her key on the marble top of his center island. Took the long way to the foyer, avoiding the living room and dining room. Grabbed her coat and purse from the hall closet. Let herself out.

And of course, had the incredible bad luck to run into Cooper as he was getting off the elevator.

"Leaving so soon?" His upper lip curled and his tone was snide.

"I had time to poison your portion," she replied as she brushed past him. "Don't worry. It won't kill you, but the toilet will be your new best friend." She wasn't fast enough to reach the elevator button and was going to have to wait for it to make the long trip back to the penthouse.

Cooper decided to wait with her.

"Why do you have it in for me and my brothers?"

"I don't. I don't know you. Except for stories Tag has told me."

"Okay, some of those stories might be prejudicial," Cooper conceded. "He actually believes you didn't set him up with the steroid story. Over his girlfriend, he believes you."

"He and Terra broke up last fall. She's changed her mind. That's only one of the many reasons she used me as her patsy. Tag believes me because he knows the truth. He was there."

Cooper kept inching closer to her, so Skye tried to put some distance between them. Not too much, though, because she didn't want to miss the elevator again. Cooper must have read her mind, because he suddenly braced one hand against the wall, blocking her off from the elevator. "Terra says you tricked Tag into proposing."

"How would she know?" Skye didn't even blink. She thought about the knives in their case and tried to judge how difficult it would be to pull one out and still surprise Cooper. "Although she did keep sneaking into our rooms, so maybe she was lurking when Tag's agent suggested a phony engagement."

Cooper blinked. "Phony engagement?"

"It's not real. It's never been real. Marty Fiscoe was just indulging in some wishful-thinking damage control."

"So the prenuptial I heard him ask for was just a ploy?"

"What?" She didn't know anything about a prenuptial. "I don't know what you're talking about." It would be just like Tag to go off and do something like that without mentioning it to her. Not that it mattered.

"But will you sign one?" Cooper asked.

"No." If she wasn't going to marry Tag, what was the point of signing a prenuptial when there would be no nuptials? "Tag doesn't have anything I want," she clarified.

The elevator chimed. Finally.

Skye ducked under Cooper's arm. "Have a nice visit."

She half expected Cooper to follow her into the car, but he stood and stared at her until the doors slid shut.

She pulled her phone out of her purse and called a cab. She hadn't driven her catering van, wanting to avoid a repeat of the previous day's press mob. Which meant she was going to have to wait in the lobby until the cab arrived.

The story of her life.

"I ran into the caterer at the elevator," Coop announced as he sauntered into the dining room. "She informed me she has no intention of signing that prenuptial agreement you asked your lawyer to draw up."

Tag glared at him. He'd never liked Coop even as a kid. The only time they'd ever gotten along was while banging Christi Fellows.

"Not a problem. I'll change my will. Cut you and the girls out." Right now his sibs stood to inherit everything. His two brothers-in-law were okay. Harper and Piper could have done worse. Coop and Hunter didn't need his millions either. The Geek and the Doc did just fine on their own.

But Red? Red could use the money. He knew how disappointed she'd been when it came time to buy her new stove that she hadn't been able to get the one she really wanted. He could have given it to her, but Red was stubborn like that. All the more reason for him to leave her his millions. Or whatever was left of them when he finally kicked. She'd get it all whether or not he got a ring on her finger.

Coop sat, spread a napkin over his lap, and helped himself to whatever the hell Red had piled on the platter. Tag had lost his appetite. If he were a drinking man, he might have been deep into a bottle of bourbon by now. But he'd seen what drowning one's sorrows in the bottom of a bottle had done to his former teammate Noah Nash. Or that might have been Noah's gambling habit and Drake Dixon's blackmail of him over it.

No woman, not even Red, was going to turn him into that kind of dissipated, useless clod of turf.

So he chewed on the ice cubes in his glass of root beer.

Hunter was eating too. "She's one fine cook. No wonder you want to marry her. What *is* this stuff?"

"Something healthy," Tag growled. "And cooking isn't why I want to marry her."

"Yeah, you got it bad," Hunter muttered before forking in another portion of the vegetable medley.

"A guilty conscious?" That was huge. And bad.

"The hots," Coop said. "Even I, in my self-absorbed quest for sex, can see how badly you want her."

Okay. So he found Red sexy. "She isn't just about sex. I could tell you a dozen great things about her and not even scratch the surface."

"She's a great cook. That's one." Hunter didn't look up from his plate. Their mother would have smacked him upside the head for his table manners—or lack thereof.

Coop snorted. "*How do I love thee? Let me count the ways.* Hunter just named one. Eleven to go."

Tag blinked. Some uncomfortable unfurled in his gut. Love? He didn't *love* Red. Not like *that*. And she didn't love him either.

"What's number two?" Coop persisted.

"She's my best friend. I can tell her anything, and she doesn't judge."

"Three?"

"She's loyal. To me." That was important. And she'd proven that loyalty repeatedly. Even to her own detriment. But he was going to make it up to her.

"So loyal she busted your steroid use to the papers. Uh-huh. I think your logic just fell apart." Coop grinned, as if this whole situation was the world's biggest joke.

"I've never knowingly used steroids in any form, and Red didn't do anything. And that's the last time I'm going to tell that to either of you."

The problem was that while he could prove he wasn't doping, he couldn't prove Red had nothing to do with the Internet story.

"I believe you about the steroids," Coop said.

"That's why I want to marry Red," Tag admitted. "To show the world that I believe her innocence."

"Whose cockamamie idea was that?" Coop again.

"Marty's," Tag admitted.

Coop snorted. "You know, she just told me that, and I didn't believe her."

Hunter stopped chewing long enough to offer: "No wonder she's giving you grief."

"She's not giving me grief. She just needs to be sensible about this."

"Whose idea was the prenup?" Coop wasn't dropping it.

"Marty's."

"No wonder women say guys only think with their dicks." Hunter put down his fork. Wiped his mouth with his napkin. "You're walking proof."

"Says the geek."

"I'm not still playing games for a living." Hunter sounded calm. Not at all judgmental. "I'm actually in a stable relationship with a woman."

"Let's talk about that instead of me."

"Coop and I didn't come to South Carolina to discuss our careers and love lives. You're the one who's splashed all over the news."

"I explained about a thousand times—none of that is true. Terra—you met her for God's sake—is a jealous, vindictive, career-hungry, man-eating bitch."

"That nice lady?" Coop asked. "She was very sweet and personable when we met for coffee earlier."

"She's a reporter. It's all an act to get you to let your guard down."

"Not that you're bitter," Coop said.

"My guard was never let down. She's dishonest. I've known it for years."

"So why were you with her so long?" Hunter asked.

"Having a steady woman is safer—sexually speaking—than groupies. I'm a healthy male. I like sex."

"So as soon as you met Skye, you threw her over." Coop held up his hands. "That's what she told me."

"I met Red at the ballpark when she started catering for the team." Even then he'd been attracted to her, asking for a good-luck kiss before every home game. "We joked around a little. Then, when I got hurt, the team hired her to cook for me while I was laid up and they were at the World Series." He could say 'World Series' now without wanting to punch someone. "And my alleged girlfriend told me she was in Wherethefuck-istan chasing down a story on missing Russian nuclear warheads or else she'd come to Columbia to take care of me."

"And if you hadn't been injured, you'd have been in Seattle playing in the series, so she had every right to pursue her own career." Coop picked up his fork and speared a chunk of chick-en.

"She wasn't in Asia minor or major. The only head, war or otherwise, was her going down on Drake Dixon and a bunch of his trust-fund cronies. And when I found out, I wasn't even jealous, because I'd gotten to know Red a whole lot better. She even stayed to watch the series on TV with me when no one else would or could. She was here for me. Not one of you, not one of my sisters, or even my parents could be bothered even to check on me. Red was here. Every day. Feeding me. Feeding my day nurse, night nurse, physical therapist."

"Feeding your soul?" Coop asked.

"Don't be a pussy."

SUNDAY, MARCH 5

Sunday morning dawned clear and a little warmer than it had been. Skye rose early and took her time getting ready for her meeting with Joel Green. She carefully packed a representative sample of some of the foods she'd been prepping for the Purim Carnival. Especially the apricot-filled hamantaschen.

She was early for her appointment.

"I like a prompt woman," Joel said as he ushered her into his office.

Skye smiled. "Some people find it a curse." She carried a platter of the delicacies she'd hand-picked to present to Joel. "I also brought some foods for you to try."

He peered through the crinkled plastic wrap. "Apricot hamantaschen. I think you're bribing me."

"Busted." She kept her tone light. Playful, but professional. Definitely not flirtatious. "I know you're concerned about my qualifications because this is your first big event, and it's not of your planning."

"It's also the first big event since the inauguration, and people are nervous," Joel said. "A non-Jewish caterer has some members wondering what you're up to."

"I appreciate your honesty. As I told you before, I'm up to trying to earn a living. I saw a need for kosher catering in this area and decided that since a great deal of it connects well with my own food philosophies, I'd go for it. I'm trying to survive as a business woman as well as trying to improve the diets of my clients."

Joel smirked. "My grandmother's liberal use of chicken fat wasn't exactly health food. She even *schmaltzed* up the vegetables."

Skye didn't let her smile fade. "No, but from what I've learned, a lot of traditional kosher dishes are based on the food of poverty, made palatable by clever and inventive cooks."

"Are you sucking up to me, Ms. Schuyler?"

"Nope. Just being honest. Take the hamantaschen, for example. Traditional fillings are dried fruits—prunes, apricots, and so on."

"Do you mind if I try one?"

"Then you trust my kosher certification?"

He paused in his struggle with the plastic wrap. "Yes. Your facilities seem up to par and I have to trust the rabbis who passed you." He plucked a cookie from the platter. Bit into it. Particles of pastry flaked around his lips. "Oh." His mouth was full when he spoke. "The sisterhoods at the temples are not going to be happy with you."

"I take it the cookie passes muster."

Joel nodded. "Have a seat. Please."

Skye lowered herself into a visitor chair. Instead of taking his place behind his desk, Joel took the other visitor's chair.

"What do you know about Purim?" he asked.

"A secretly Jewish queen saved the Jews from being massacred. She dolled up and invited the king to a banquet."

Joel smiled. "That's part of it."

"I like strong women. Is there a reason for this?"

"Jewish Community Centers around the country have seen an increase in threats over the past several months. Based on our history, we're concerned."

Dread iced over her insides. But she wasn't going to pussyfoot around the topic. "Are you breaking your contract with me?"

"No. No."

She thought the denial might have come a bit too quickly.

"I've put a lot of work and money into the food." She'd busted her butt before the Gems called her to Florida. "I've made hundreds of mini potato and kasha knishes. My freezer is filled with kosher hot dogs. I've placed the order for hot dog buns. Oh, and I'm making latkes to serve with homemade apple sauce—I know that's more of a Chanukah food, but it's still tasty and festive." She knew she was babbling, but she couldn't stop. She needed this job. Sure, she could sue for breach of contract, but she didn't have the money to do that either.

"Would the local rabbis feel more confident if they quizzed me on the holiday?" God. She sounded desperate. Bad move on her part. Never let them see you sweat? She might as well be drenched, so that was another rule down the drain.

"There are subtleties it wouldn't hurt you to know."

"Like?"

Joel crossed his legs. "The hamantaschen pastries. Do you know what the word means?"

"Haman's hat. I'll confess that I don't understand that. I thought Haman was the villain of the story. Isn't that why every time his name is mentioned during the reading of the Megillah Purim it's booed? "

Joel grinned. "Or drowned out with groggers."

"Noisemakers. So if he's the villain, why his hat?"

"Linguistics. Originally the word was *manatashen*—or poppy seed. It somehow morphed into hamantaschen. It's said the three-cornered shape of the pastry is shaped like the hat Haman wore."

"So it's more a tradition than something with religious meaning."

"Correct. Judaism is rich in tradition. We have a long history."

"And if some of my pastries end up with four corners instead of three, that won't be grounds to not pay me?"

Joel laughed. "Not at all. Just don't let someone from one of the sisterhoods see them." He helped himself to another apricot cookie. "These are really good."

"Like mom used to make?"

He laughed. "No. My mother couldn't cook. But she could buy. How about your mother?"

"She died when I was eight. I don't remember very much about her."

"I'm sorry."

Skye shrugged. "Not your fault."

"So what got you interested in cooking?"

"I took care of my father. That included making sure he ate. I discovered I really enjoyed planning meals, mixing and matching textures and tastes. I like taking care of people by feeding them."

"That sounds like a Jewish mother stereotype. You know, *so eat already.*"

She smiled even though she had no idea what he was talking about.

"Well, I've taken enough of your time today," Joel said.

Skye set the platter of goodies on the corner of his desk before standing.

"You know, I don't think you need to understand the nuances of the holiday," Joel said. "Only enough of the background to...appreciate why there's some concern over your non-Jewish heritage."

"That's fair." Just because she didn't like something didn't mean it wasn't fair.

"And, unfortunately, there's that whole exposé thing with Tag Gentry. Never sabotage a local hero. But I've reassured people that Gentry doesn't seem to think you're guilty. Very fortuitous that he showed up while I was inspecting your facilities."

"Fortuitous," she echoed, sourness filling her mouth. Thanks to Terra, Tag was going to be forever linked to her life. If she managed to have one.

Tag was waiting for Skye in the alley behind Skye's the Limit.

"Should you be driving so much?" she asked as she climbed out of her van. Driving had severely impaired his bad leg only a week earlier, while they'd been in New Orleans.

"Short distances don't matter," he replied. He followed her to the door. "How did your meeting go?"

She stared at him for a moment before remembering he'd been hanging around when she took the phone call from Joel. She inserted the key in the lock. Leaned against the door to align the tumblers. "Fine. It was all about you." Only a slight exaggeration.

"What? They want me to sign baseballs at the carnival?"

Skye resisted the urge to roll her eyes. "Not quite." She tried turning the key, but it wouldn't budge. "It was more of 'gosh-he's-still-speaking-to-you-maybe-you're-not-a-horrible-person' conversation."

She tried the key again.

"You need some lube. Let me try." Tag covered her hand with his. A spring breeze drifted down the alley, bringing with it the stench of rotting garbage. Her small Dumpster should have been emptied the day before, but from the look—and the smell—that hadn't happened. She'd have to call the hauler with whom she'd contracted.

Tag finally jiggled the door open. Not good. He usually wasn't around when she was entering or exiting her building. She should use the profits from the Purim Carnival to pay a locksmith.

"So why the visit?" she asked as she opened her refrigerator. A glass of unsweetened iced tea would hit the spot. She poured two glasses, but warned Tag about the lack of sugar. He grimaced like the true southerner he was, but drank down half a glass without complaining.

"My brother said you told him you wouldn't sign a prenuptial agreement," he said once his glass was empty.

Skye sipped her tea. "So? It's a moot point. We're not getting married."

Tag scrubbed his face with his palms. He hadn't shaven. Black whiskers shadowed the lower half of his face. His gray eyes were bloodshot, as if he were hungover or suffering from sleep deprivation. "It doesn't matter whether you marry me or not. I'm changing my will. You get everything."

She slammed her glass to the counter. "What?" Surely she could not have heard him correctly.

"I'm changing my will and leaving everything to you," he repeated. "So a prenup doesn't matter whether we're married or not."

"You can't do that." He was insane. His leg injury must have knocked something loose in his head.

"Sure I can. It's my money. My brother's don't need it. My sisters have husbands of their own to provide for their kids. Who else would I leave my money too?"

"Tripp Shaneybrook," she blurted, feeling somewhat grateful she had a ready answer. "He has that camp up in Cooperstown. Baseball as a life skill. Give it to him."

"He has his own money."

Skye recognized the stubborn set of Tag's chin.

He slid off his stool. Got down on one knee—his good one. Pulled something from his pants pocket.

The kitchen started tilting. This wasn't happening. This couldn't possibly be happening. Why didn't he just wrench her heart from her chest and fandango on it?

He flipped open the black velvet jewelers' box and held it out to her. "Celeste Schuyler, will you marry me?"

She couldn't even see his face for the film of tears obstructing her vision. Tears she refused to shed over Tag Gentry.

"Why are you doing this?" She barely choked out the words. It was as if the beautiful diamond solitaire nestled against the black velvet was wrapped around her neck, strangling her. "We have nothing in common. You want adventure. I want roots." *You don't love me.*

"We can work things out. We're good at that."

"I'm good at giving in to you," she answered. "And I'm tired of that. Maybe you should leave."

Something flashed across his face. Something stark. As if she'd started gutting him while he was alive and awake. As if he couldn't believe she was turning down marriage to the great Tag Gentry.

Well, she knew the real Tucker Alexander Gentry. His eating preferences. His television viewing habits. His reverence for baseball and irreverence for anything else in life.

He didn't say anything else. Didn't argue. Didn't try to convince her. Just grabbed the stool he'd vacated and used it to pull himself upright. He then placed the ring box, still open, on the counter. Grabbed her shoulders, pulled her to her feet and pulled her close.

She didn't resist his kiss. How could she? His mouth was hot on hers. Searing. Burning straight through the layers of her resistance. Melting her bones along with her resolve.

Then he stopped.

"Think about that." His voice was raspy, and his breathing uneven. "I'll stop by tomorrow. Unless you change your mind before then. You know where to find me."

Then he was gone. He simply opened the door and walked out.

Skye slumped against the counter.

Was loving him the way she did ever going to be enough?

No. Because she deserved more. Deserved someone who was going to love her unconditionally, something she hadn't had since her mother's death.

The kiss was exactly why she couldn't see him again.

MONDAY, MARCH 6

The first thing Skye did upon waking on Monday morning was to call her trash hauler about the missed pickup. The last thing she wanted in the alley was rats.

"Your contract has been cancelled."

"What? Why?" That made no sense. "I've already paid for this month."

"Your check is being returned to you."

"But why?"

"Don't need a reason, but it seems you have a bad habit of spreading garbage around, and not one of our drivers wants to service your account."

"I have no idea what you're talking about. I'm referring to Skye's the Limit." She gave the receptionist her address. Her garbage was always bagged and tied before it went into the Dumpster. Unless someone was sneaking into her alley and leaving their trash. But she'd seen no indication of extraneous leavings.

No matter how hard she cajoled, argued, or negotiated, the company wouldn't change its mind about her account.

So time she should have spent working on recipes or baking for the Purim Carnival was instead spent trying to track down a replacement garbage hauler. Everyone was interested and wanted her business until she mentioned her name.

She put her phone down on the butcher block and stared at it. Maybe she was being paranoid or maybe the city of Columbia was out to get her for smearing Tag's reputation. Which she hadn't done.

His fans would never believe her.

Several calls had come in while she'd been trying to track down new sanitation services. Her voice mail showed four messages. She started listening. Her stomach clenched, forcing the tea she'd drunk into her throat, burning with the addition of acid.

The nasty calls had tapered off the day after Terra's story first hit the web. Now they were back with a vengeance. Maybe Terra had done another story after seeing Skye's the Limit's van parked near Tag's apartment. Or someone else, looking for their fifteen minutes of fame was piggybacking on Skye's new notoriety. Either way, the filth on her phone stole her breath. People *hated* her.

She was lucky she still had the Purim Carnival, because she doubted she would ever sign another catering contract with anyone else. Ever. Unless she changed the name of her company. Her own name. Two other messages were of the same nature. The fourth message was a cancellation of the only other job left on her calendar, along with a request for the return of the deposit.

Tag's diamond ring winked at her from the counter, as if to say, *Isn't this a great joke?*

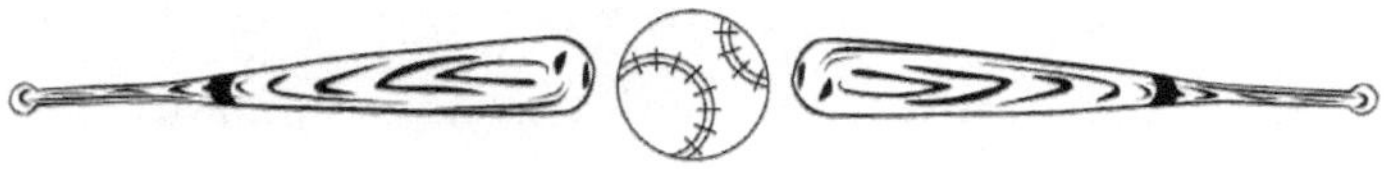

Tag's brothers departed. They had their oh-so-important lives needing them—Hunter working on the Mission to Mars and Coop his patients, all of whom wanted better breasts. And Tag was happy to see them go. They usually got along much better than they had on this trip. Of course, they usually weren't mucking around in his business either.

Now he could focus on Red. He hadn't been prepared for her to refuse a ring outright. He had to find some way to get through to her without turning into a stalker.

"Why are you so determined to marry her?" Hunter asked. "Unless you love her."

Coop didn't contradict Hunter's observation.

What the hell did he know about love? All he knew was that he wanted to hang with Red even when hanging didn't involve sex. The sex blew the top of his head off, but it wasn't everything. Did that mean he was in love with her?

He didn't think so. Maybe the thought of his brothers—or anyone else—having sex with her made him want to take a baseball bat to their dicks, followed by their heads, meant something.

Sharing a woman meant nothing. Never had. Except when it came to Red. But that didn't mean love. *Did it?* Wasn't that just some kind of sick possessiveness?

Didn't matter. Not really. He didn't want Red in bed, against a wall, or in a shower with anyone except him.

Now he just had to convince her.

But how? Trying to date her didn't work. She hadn't even blinked at the diamond solitaire. How could she be with him the way she'd been and just not give a damn?

There had to be something else going on with her. There usually was. When they'd first met, she'd been struggling to make a balloon mortgage payment, a fact he'd stumbled on purely by accident.

So what could be the bug up her gorgeous independent butt this time?

The sound of tinkling glass in the stillness of the night raised the hairs on Skye's nape and on her arms. She'd just turned off her lamp and punched her pillow in an effort to get comfortable.

The only time glass tinkled was when it was breaking. She knew that.

Her apartment was on the third floor of the Skye's the Limit building. The neighborhood consisted of strictly business premises, most of them long abandoned. She might even be living in her building illegally, but she'd worry about that when someone complained. But the deserted state of the streets meant she had few human neighbors. Even bums didn't frequent her block. She was thinking about adopting a feral cat to deal with the rat problem. The bakery at the end of the street had had great success with that strategy.

But rats didn't break glass. At least, not so that she could hear it. And this had been very clear.

If she called the cops, she'd feel foolish if someone was breaking windows next door. But what if it wasn't next door? She needed to keep a hammer or something next to her bed. Maybe she could borrow a bat from Tag.

No. No contacting Tag.

Except right now she wished she wasn't alone. In the dark. In a creaky old building. With people sending threats to her. The garbage guys might be only the first of a lot of bad crap.

She climbed out of bed. Pulled on her robe and shoved her feet into the pair of flip-flops she used as slippers. She used the flashlight app on her phone to light her way, aiming it at the floor so no one outside could see it through one of the dusty windows. The stair treads groaned beneath her weight, no matter how lightly she tried to step. Her slippers slapped against her heels. Some sneak she was. She kicked them off.

She strained to hear if anything else was happening downstairs, but the thudding of her blood against her eardrums drowned out everything but the noise she was making. Everything on the second floor was quiet and as it should be. As far as she could tell. Someday she hoped to turn the space into a banquet facility, but tonight it was a yawning mouth of darkness, threatening to consume her courage. She willed her legs to stop trembling. She was an adult. She could do this.

The stairs to the second floor were a little less cantankerous.

The stairwell was located between the kitchen and the space that had once housed the dining room of a restaurant. Skye paused. Pinkish light filtered through a gap in the dusty drapes covering the even dustier oversized windows. A finger of cool air brushed her cheek.

Something was open. She'd locked up, being extra careful since returning from New Orleans, before she'd gone upstairs. But night air was reaching through some opening, grasping at her.

She backed up two steps, sat and hid her phone in her robe before dialing 9-1-1. The light filtered through the aqua cotton as if it were birthing a hobgoblin.

She spoke as quietly as she could. Gave her address. Said she thought someone had broken in. The 9-1-1 operator stayed on the phone with her. Which was good.

Breathing was hard. The pressure in her chest wasn't letting her do much of anything. Even when she saw the strobing blue and red of the police cruiser lights, she was afraid to move. "Ms. Schuyler!" someone called out.

Skye managed to climb to her feet.

"The officers have arrived," the operator told her. "They're at the front door."

Damn. She should have told them to come to the back. She stood and went into the abandoned dining area. Stepped on something sharp and painful and couldn't help but yelp.

Pounding on the front door resumed.

"I'm coming!" she said. The key hung on a spike to the left of the door, where it couldn't be reached by someone breaking a window. Every step stabbed something deeper into her foot. She turned on the overhead lights and unlocked the door.

A uniformed officer entered. Brady, according to his name badge. "Are you all right?"

"I stepped on something." She supposed she should have asked for ID before letting him in, but she was scared.

He turned on his flashlight and shone it on her foot. "You're bleeding."

Yes. She was.

"It looks as if your front window was broken."

Hard for her to tell because of the draperies.

"Do you need an ambulance?"

She shook her head. Who could afford one?

Brady offered his arm and led her to one of the wobbly tables and even wobblier chairs. He knelt before her. Shone his light on her foot. "Looks like a sliver of glass."

The floor was covered with shards, splinters, and chips. The window was old, probably original to the building, and old glass didn't break the way newer stuff did.

"You're going to need an ambulance."

"No. Really."

"Then call someone to drive you to the ER. This is nothing to mess with." He stood and started looking around, using his high-powered beam to illuminate the damage because the overhead fixtures were as filthy as everything else in this room.

Call someone. Right. She didn't have friends; she had clients. And Tag. Who was a client. A former friend.

It was either him or the expense of an ambulance.

Tag was brooding in his living room, staring at Japanese badminton finals on an obscure cable sports network, when Red's name flashed on his phone. Something weird happened in his chest. He'd sworn he was going to give her space and time, but here she was. Relief. That was what he felt.

"Tag? Can you come over?" Red's voice was shaky. "I need your help. If you can. If you can't, that's okay."

She needed his help? Red swore she never needed anything from anyone. This had to be dire. Or maybe she just needed help being convinced they ought to get married.

"No, I'll be right over."

He wasn't sure, but he thought he heard her say *thank you*.

The twenty minutes between his penthouse and her ramshackle building had never seemed so long. The traffic lights ganged up on him. He hit every red. He considered running a few of them, but with the way life had been conspiring against him lately, he'd be caught. No point feeding the scandalmongers anything else.

Except when he turned onto Red's street and saw the police cruiser parked in front of her building. The gossip rags and faux journalists would have a field day with what was going to happen to anyone who messed with Red.

Since the lights were on in the front of the building, that was where he parked. One of the big plate glass windows was no longer intact. A good-sized jagged-edged hole was clearly visible from the street.

That was going to need to be fixed as quickly as possible. Too bad his brothers weren't still in town. Their farm-learned carpentry skills might be rusty, but between the three of them, they could have boarded over the window until Red could have it replaced.

He knocked on the door, which was opened by a uniformed officer.

Dear God, there was blood. Everywhere. "Tag Gentry." The cop recognized him immediately. Not unusual here in Columbia.

Tag ignored him and hurried to Red's side. Because of the blood. Her foot, wrapped in a towel, was coated. Dripped on the floor. Glass crunched under his shoes. He squatted next to her. Grabbed her hand. It was icy. "What the fuck happened? Are you okay?"

"Someone threw a brick through the window," she said. She sounded weak. Maybe she'd lost too much blood.

"Where are your shoes?"

"Where were you earlier tonight?" the officer asked.

"What?" Tag asked at the same time as Red.

The cop's hand hovered over the butt of his service revolver. "Where were you about an hour ago?"

"At home," Tag replied.

"Oh for crying out loud," Red said. "You told me to call someone to take me to the emergency room. Now you're interrogating him?"

"You need the ER?" Tag's attention immediately returned to Red.

"I have slivers of glass in my soles," she said.

"Why didn't you call an ambulance?" Tag nearly bellowed the question. But he was glad she'd reached out to him. That had to mean something. Didn't it?

"If you think about it, you'll know why. Officer Brady suggested I call a friend." She sounded hurt. Not physically because of her foot, but because Tag was acting like a jerk.

"Okay. It's good you called me." He glared at the cop. "I was home, watching TV. No alibi."

"Tag didn't do this."

"He has motivation." The cop's tone was flat. "Even if you do deserve some vandalism."

Red grabbed Tag's arm before he could be brought up on charges of assaulting an officer.

"A little prejudiced?" he asked instead.

The cop looked momentarily confused.

"Why would I smash my fiancée's window?"

"Fiancée?"

"It's a French word meaning the woman I'm going to marry." He glanced at the hand he still held. No ring. "Why aren't you wearing your ring?"

Instead of answering, she busied herself refolding the towel loosely draped over her foot.

"How can you marry her after what she did to you?" the cop blurted.

"What did she do to me? Refuse to spend the night at my place?" Tag stroked Red's palm.

"Can you think of anyone who might have it in for you?" the cop asked Red.

The look she gave him could have withered an outfield. "Can you think of anyone besides Tag who doesn't?"

The cop had the grace to look uncomfortable. He resumed asking questions Red couldn't answer as he filled out his report.

Tag released her hand and wandered to the kitchen. The diamond solitaire was right where he'd left it that afternoon. He was good enough to call in an emergency but not good enough to marry. Resentment nipped at him.

He scooped up the ring box, then snooped around the first floor a little more. Looking for other damage. Not only because he didn't fully trust the cop, but because he really hadn't seen much of the place. He found her cubbyhole of an office and grabbed the rolling chair. If his leg were one hundred percent, he could have carried her to his car without even blinking. She'd never be able to walk with glass embedded in her sole. So the desk chair would have to substitute for a wheelchair.

Then he called Marty. Okay, it was the middle of the night, but Marty was used to coddling his clients. That was what a good agent did. At least in Tag's mind. He explained the situation, then added, "I need someone to board over the window now while I take her to hospital."

Marty grumbled, but he was a whiz at making things happen.

Tag found the cop ready to leave when he rolled the chair to the dining room. "I'll file the report."

"See that you do." Tag kept his tone cool as he grabbed Red's left hand again and jammed the engagement ring on her finger. "You shouldn't leave it next to the sink," he lied for the cop's benefit. "It could fall down the drain."

He brought her hand to his mouth. Brushed his lips across her knuckles.

As soon as the cop was gone, Red snatched her hand away from him. "Nice show."

"Yeah, well, how quick do you think we'll get processed at the emergency room as the woman who announced to the world that I'm on steroids, compared to the woman who is my fiancée?"

"I'm not going to the hospital," she said. "I have tweezers. There's better light in the kitchen."

She started to stand, but he grasped her biceps and pulled her into the rolling chair.

"Great idea. Thanks."

She seemed to be under some misguided impression that he was going to enable her.

"Where are you going?" she asked as he rolled her toward the front door.

"My car." He kept his voice as emotionless as possible. "You don't think I'm wheeling your chair all the way to St. Bruno's, do you?"

"The kitchen is in the opposite direction. I'm not going to the ER."

"Yeah? How do you think you're going to get out of it?" He noticed the old-fashioned key dangling from the lock of the front door. He yanked it out.

"I can't afford a hospital visit," she said in a low voice. Maybe she was afraid the ghosts of the neighborhood might hear her.

"I can. And don't argue. You call me in the middle of night, you don't get a say in how I react."

"You said you were watching TV," she reminded him. "You don't get a say in my life."

"Until you call me for help." Reminders worked two ways.

He opened his car door, then braced himself to lift her onto the seat. Mentally cursed his bum leg. "What the hell are you wearing?"

He'd just noticed her robe. And he was intimately familiar with her usual skimpy sleepwear.

"I was in bed when I heard the glass break. I can't go to the hospital dressed like this."

"Sure you can. They'll only put you in something worse when you get there. Don't sweat it. So why didn't you put on slippers or your flip-flops?" He reached across her to fasten her seat belt, but she slapped at his hands.

"I did have on my flip-flops. But they were making too much noise when I walked down the stairs, so I kicked them off."

"You went to check on the sound of broken glass before you called the cops? What kind of special stupid are you? Don't answer that." He probably would have done the same thing.

He walked around the front of the SUV. Struggled to climb in, but managed.

They didn't speak again until they were nearly at the hospital.

"I'm paying. No arguments," he said. "You're my fiancée. Again, don't argue about this."

Maybe she was finally realizing the benefits she would enjoy as Mrs. Tag Gentry. She should.

At least she kept his ring on her finger. He called ahead for a wheelchair. The hospital was happy to do anything for Tag Gentry's future wife. His name was still as good as a magic wand.

Until Red checked in. She was a goddess until she said her name. Or maybe it was Tag's paranoia that made the woman asking the questions seem so cool. So distant.

Red might have told him that was only his ego talking.

Except the clerk raised an eyebrow when Tag produced his gold card for payment. Red had the good sense to keep her mouth shut. To respond to the questions in a monotone. In monosyllabic words when she could get away with it.

The only good thing to come out of the check-in procedure was he learned when her birthday was. He tapped the date into his phone.

There was so much he still had to learn about her.

At least she'd called him when she needed someone. He found solace in that.

"What do you mean I have to stay off my feet?" Skye asked the doctor.

The doctor, who in no way resembled any handsome TV doctor since the advent of TV doctors, repeated his instructions. "You need to give your feet a chance to heal."

When she did something, she didn't do it halfway. Both feet had slivers and chips of glass. Her right foot was the worst and really hurt. Most of the blood in the dining room and probably Tag's car came from those cuts.

"I have a business to run," she said, swallowing her panic. The remnants of a business. But if she could pull off the Purim Carnival, some of the attendees might keep her in mind when they were looking for a caterer for their bar mitzvahs and weddings.

The doctor shrugged. "I'm just trying to help you. But if pain is your thing, go for it."

"I'll see to it she stays off her feet," Tag said. He grinned. "I owe her."

She wasn't speaking to him. If she were, she might ask him *for what?* She hadn't cared for him when he'd hurt his leg. She'd cooked for him. He'd had day and night nurses.

The first thing Tag did was stop at a 24-hour pharmacy and purchase her a new pair of flip-flops.

She broke her vow never to speak to him again when he didn't take her back to Skye's the Limit. "I need to go home," she said. "I have to call someone to board up the window, clean up the glass and blood, and I have an event in five days."

Tag pulled into the underground parking garage of his building. "The window and cleanup are being taken care of. You're spending the rest of the night with me. You know, a place where people aren't heaving bricks at you."

"No one heaved a brick at me," she muttered. "There's a difference between vandalism and assault."

"And I'm not taking any chances with your safety."

"It was probably random," she said. If she stayed with Tag, she knew what would happen. Her nipples were already reacting to her unwanted memories of Tag's mouth. His fingers. His dick.

"The neighborhood isn't that great again yet." Tag yanked the key from the ignition.

"But it will be. And Skye's the Limit is going to be one of the pioneers making it so." If she could hold on that long.

Tag got out of the car and took her new crutches from the cargo area before opening the passenger door.

What a great couple they made, both limping on their right sides.

Skye managed on the crutches into the garage elevator to the lobby. Across the lobby to the elevator that would whisk them to Tag's penthouse.

He didn't ask her if she wanted a guest room. He simply steered her to his room. Led her to his bed. Sat her on the edge of the mattress before taking away her crutches once again.

"Finally got you where I want you," he murmured as he sat next to her.

They hadn't been together since New Orleans. Tag cupped her cheek in his oversized palm. His calluses scraped her skin. "I am very glad you called me tonight. It gives me hope."

Not this again. Please.

"I didn't know who else to call," she confessed. And what did it say about her that she'd been in Columbia for nearly two years and had one friend?

Tag's mouth covered hers before she could mention that fact to him. She parted her lips for his tongue. It was like striking a match. One moment Tag was gentle. Hesitant. The next he pulled at her clothes. Knew exactly how to rid her of her robe, her fleece running shorts, and the oversized sleep shirt burying her upper torso. She was naked before she could even start unbuttoning the placket of his pale yellow golf shirt. He didn't wait for her to begin but shucked his clothes as quickly as he could. His body was warm, his skin almost painfully hot against hers. His mouth was demanding, and she gave as good as she got. Her nipples were diamond tips. And she was wet. Drenched. Tag had barely touched her.

"What say we skip a condom tonight?" he asked.

Talk about a mood killer. "What say we don't," she replied. "What is wrong with you?"

Tag brushed his hand over her belly. "I wouldn't mind starting our family."

"Family?" Skye jackknifed to a sitting position. She didn't want a family. Not with Tag. She was the poster child for what an emotionally absentee father could do to a kid. She wasn't going to put her children through that. If she ever had them. The father of *her* children would love her and their offspring.

"Yeah. I want a couple of kids. Not as many as my folks, but a couple."

She couldn't believe what she was hearing. "This engagement is fake, or have you forgotten?"

"I'm serious. I don't know why you think I'm not."

"Because your agent suggested we do this as a public relations stunt." Talk about getting a girl out of the mood. The diamond on her finger winked in the dim lamplight of Tag's bedroom. She started to pull the ring from her finger, but Tag stopped her.

"Maybe Marty suggested it as such, but the more I think about it, the more I realize it's a great idea."

A great idea. Whatever happened to love? Forsaking all others? She didn't want a marriage of convenience. She'd told him she didn't much like that trope in romance novels. Unless it was well done. Very well done. Believable. But Marty's suggestion smacked of contrivance.

"A wife will only bog you down," she said. Maybe if she made it more about him on the negative side, he'd see reason. It was all about him when it came to the advantages of marriage. Besides, he could marry anyone he wanted.

Tag tugged on her arm. Pulled her onto his chest. "You wouldn't bog me down. You get me."

"I would bog you down." She was firm. "I'm not a wanderer. I want roots."

"Like I said. You get me."

"But you don't get me."

Something flashed in his eyes. Maybe surprise. "I get you." His voice was low. Rough. He rolled over, pulling her with him. He had the advantage now, with her on her back, looking up at him. "I've got you right now."

He lowered his head. Claimed her mouth, searing his way straight through to her soul.

A moment later he nuzzled her neck and said, "In another thirty seconds, I'm going to take you."

Before she could say anything, he stretched for his nightstand drawer. Fished out a condom. Rolled it down his erection.

Then he was inside her. Thrusting deeply. And it not only felt good, it felt right. She let her reservations fall away. Be driven underground by the force of Tag's fucking.

It would be so easy to just give in and marry him. Except she wanted forever, and Tag wasn't a forever kind of guy. Except maybe when it came to baseball. He'd planned to play forever. Planned to be a Columbia Gem forever. Everything else was merely an obstacle. And that was his problem. His forever was ending, and he couldn't admit it.

"Aren't you going to come?" he asked.

Usually all he had to do was look at her and her orgasm was right there. But the numbing agent the ER doctor had used on her foot was wearing off. Her heel hurt. She was concerned about her building and the broken window. And she loved Tag so damn much it pained her. She didn't know how she could ever escape the spell he seemed to have cast on her.

"Don't worry about me," she murmured.

"There are two of us in this bed. We're both supposed to be having a good time."

She nipped at his collarbone. The slightly salty tang of his skin on her tongue was ambrosia. "I'm fine."

"I worry about you all the time." He pushed into her. "Especially lately."

"You shouldn't," she replied as he withdrew. She gasped when he thrust again.

"Do I bore you?" he asked.

"No!"

"Should I get my brothers back here to help fuck you? They certainly made it clear they wouldn't mind a piece of you."

She tried to slap his face, but he grabbed her hands before she connected. He easily gripped her wrists in one huge hand and held them over her head.

"Admit it. You've been curious ever since I told you about Christi Fellows when we were in New Orleans."

"No." She didn't even much like his brothers.

"Well, let me tell you something, Red. I am not sharing you. Not with my brothers, not with Terra, and not with your horny clients."

He withdrew completely, leaving her empty and vaguely achy.

The harsh kiss that followed drove every thought from her head. The scruff on his face scraped her skin as he worked his mouth away from hers and down her jaw. Tag used his tongue—so hot and wet—to trace the rim of her ear before drawing her lobe into his mouth and sucking.

He was going to force a climax from her, even if it killed her.

Like when his dragged his mouth to the side of her neck. He'd spent weeks learning every pleasure point on her body; now he was putting that knowledge into seducing her. She shuddered as his nibbled the cord between ear and shoulder. The arching of her spine was completely involuntary, but he must have mistaken it for an invitation, because he abandoned her neck to nip his way to her breasts.

Oh, the things that man could do to a nipple with his mouth should have been illegal.

"I ought to handcuff you to the headboard," he muttered. His breath heated her flesh. "Tie you up and work you over until you say, *Yes, Tag, I will marry you.*"

This insane statement ended with him nursing at her breast, the deep, rhythmic sucking punctuated by visits from his teeth.

Skye curled her fingers around the iron bars of his headboard. Tried to swallow a moan, but failed.

Tag released her nipple. "I heard that." His voice was as rough as his unshaven cheeks. "Now I'm going to make you scream."

He kissed his way down her ribs, across her belly, stopping a moment at her navel.

She wanted to scream, *stop!* She wanted to run as far away from him as she could get. At least, her brain did. But her body betrayed her. Her thighs separated, seemingly of their own volition, as she dug her heels into the mattress.

"I love that you don't shave or wax your pussy. I don't want to fuck a little girl, but a woman. My woman." His humid breath ruffled her pubic hair.

Then he delved. He homed in on her clit with his tongue. A few more licks before he applied suction.

Skye released the headboard and reached for Tag's head. She burrowed her fingers through his soft hair to his scalp. Clutched his skull. The faint vibration against her clit might have been a chuckle. Her moans turned to cries. Flashes of heat seared her soles, flickered up her calves and thighs.

He inserted one large finger into her as he continued to use his mouth. The thrusting mimicked fucking, and she found herself moving in tandem. When he eased a a second finger into her ass, she gave up trying to think.

The orgasm she thought had deserted her exploded. As Tag had threatened, she screamed. Shudders wracked her body.

The next thing she knew, Tag abandoned her pussy. He crawled up her body. She wrapped her arms around him as an anchor and locked her legs around his waist.

"That's right. Come for me. Keep coming for me." He wasn't gentle when he shoved his penis into her. She didn't want him to be. A second climax rode the wave of the first.

"Has anyone else ever fucked you like this?" He still thrust. Still tried to fuck another orgasm out of her. She smelled the scent of her arousal on his lower face.

"No. God, no." Because she'd never loved anyone before. Never wanted to crawl inside someone and stay there forever, sharing breath and heartbeat. Had never let herself become so vulnerable to someone's whims and moods before.

"Good. And you know what else? They never will."

"Because you're the almighty Tag Gentry?"

"No. Because I'm your man."

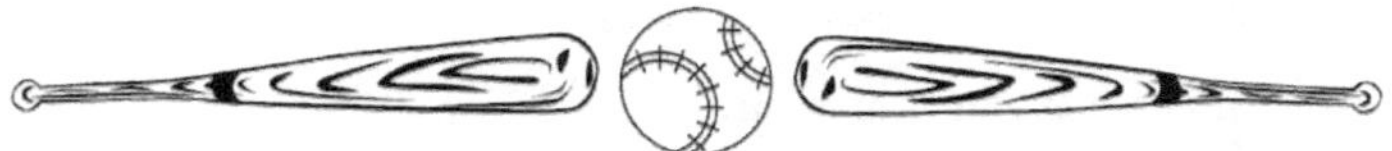

Tag lay on his back, staring at the darkness overhead. Red sprawled next him, breathing deeply as she slept, not quite snoring, but releasing little ruffles of air.

He was amazed she was asleep. Amazed she wasn't feigning slumber, waiting until he succumbed so she could press a pillow against his face and smother him. If their roles were reversed, he'd be tempted.

He didn't understand what had gotten into him. Couldn't explain how her lack of response had gotten under his skin. More than hurt pride was involved.

She'd reached out to him when she needed someone only because he was the one person she knew. He didn't understand any of her distance. It wasn't something that had started in New Orleans, but before. New Orleans had brought them closer together. Everything they'd been through had been resolved because they had each other's backs.

Until Marty had mentioned the fake engagement.

Okay, he got that Red was so honest that kind of lie wouldn't sit well with her. But he'd offered to make the deal genuine. Had tried to spend non-fucking time with her. Had gotten down on one knee—him with only one working knee—and presented a ring.

What more did she want?

His gut feared she wanted his brothers. He never should have told her about the nympho neighbor who'd fuck anyone and maybe anything. He'd given Red ideas. Ideas he didn't want her to have. She could deny it all she wanted, but he'd seen how she avoided Hunter and Coop, afraid they'd see her curiosity and her desire. Maybe that was what they'd reacted to—Red's unspoken lust for them.

Well, he didn't need help making his woman come. He'd just proven it, and his cock seemed to be thinking about trying to prove it again. Except she was definitely asleep. He knew the signs. She needed her sleep. She had work to do. He knew how hard she worked preparing for an event. This carnival at the Jewish Community Center was bigger than anything he'd known her to do. Yes, bigger than catering a World Series game. Maybe more important, because at the stadium she was anonymous except to the players and staff. At the JCC people would ask who had provided the food. Her name would be in the program—*Catering by Skye's the Limit.* She could get new clients, work other events.

But he hated seeing her work so hard—and for nothing. She'd busted her ass over the World Series and the Gems had yet to renew her contract, even with the added incentive of a blackmail recording of the majority stockholder attempting sexual assault. She'd busted her ass over Dixon's Halloween party too. She'd even slaved for Noah Nash's imaginary Mardi Gras ball when she still planned to leave. Red was a worker.

He leaned down and brushed his lips across her forehead. Her skin was cool. The fruity scent of her shampoo tickled his nostrils. This. He wanted this. Marriage to Red would give him this.

Funny. He'd never had these imaginings with Terra or any other woman in his life, and there had been quite a few. Never one who insinuated herself so deeply into his space though. He preferred the female's space—he could leave on his agenda. Didn't have to think about her because she wasn't around. That was his usual form of relationship. Everything with Red had been different from the beginning.

If he hadn't gotten involved with Red, and Terra had shown up while his brothers were visiting, they all could have a good time. A real good time. Tag wouldn't have blinked.

He didn't want Coop or Hunter even looking at Red.

Maybe that should worry him.

But it didn't.

WEDNESDAY, MARCH 8

Officer Brady was at Skye's the Limit the next morning when Skye finally convinced Tag he either drive her home or she would call a cab or walk. Someone from the police department had called her cell phone and asked her to be there.

Skye was surprised to see Brady. He'd made it pretty clear the previous night that her building could blow up and, as far as he was concerned, it would be only what she had coming to her.

The broken front window was boarded over. Whoever Tag had nudged had been quick.

"Can't let you in," Brady said.

"Why not?" Skye asked. If it was another gas leak, like she'd had at Halloween, she was screwed. "How soon before I can get in?"

Brady skimmed her scanty clothing, his gaze heating.

She tugged her robe tighter, while Tag practically growled at the officer.

"We got a call," Brady said.

"About what? A gas leak? Did someone call SCG&E?"

"Not a gas leak. A dead body."

The skin on Skye's arms prickled. The morning was warm for early March, so she wasn't chilled by the weather.

"Inside or out?" She was amazed she could ask the question in such a calm tone of voice.

Brady narrowed his eyes at her.

Tag's hand rested on the small of her back.

"Because if it's outside, you might want to check my Dumpster. My trash pick-up company cancelled my contract without notice earlier this week, so the garbage is a little ripe."

"I need to get into the building."

"Do you have a search warrant?" Tag asked.

Brady glanced away from Skye.

Under normal circumstances, she would have let the police in and let them look around.

"Tag's right, Officer Brady. Anyone could have climbed through the broken window last night while I was at the hospital and planted God knows what. It's not as if this neighborhood is teeming with potential witnesses."

"Warrant is on its way."

Skye swayed. She still wasn't steady on her feet, one of which throbbed like crazy. If not for Tag's supporting hand, she might have toppled over.

"Can she go in?" Tag asked.

Brady crossed his arms over his chest. "No."

Tag cupped her elbow and helped her back to his car. Helped her climb into the passenger seat.

"Where are you going?" Brady asked.

"She needs to sit," Tag snapped. He slammed the door before walking around the front of his vehicle and climbing in next to her.

"Do you have a lawyer?"

"Not really." Unfortunately, it sounded as if she was going to need one. And pay one.

Tag pulled out his phone. Hit a single button. "Marty? Thanks for taking care of Red's window last night. We have another problem. The cops are waiting on a search warrant to ransack her place of business. They won't tell us why. She needs a lawyer. Now." He disconnected the call.

Skye buried her face in her hands. Rubbed her eyes with the heels of her palms as if that would erase the thoughts clamoring for attention in her brain.

"You're not crying, are you?" Tag's tone was hesitant.

She shook her head. Dropped her hands so he could witness her tearless state. He took her left hand, the one still adorned with his ring, and held it. "Marty is getting us a lawyer. A criminal lawyer."

"I can't pay a lawyer." Her voice was stronger than she felt.

"I'm paying the lawyer."

"No. This isn't a *we* situation. This is just me, losing everything I've worked to build."

"That's where you're wrong. This crap is happening because of me, and I don't shirk my responsibilities."

Just what she wanted to hear: she was a responsibility. She tried to tug her hand from his grip, but he wasn't letting go.

"You wouldn't be in this mess if you weren't trying to help me. You wouldn't be in this mess if I'd handled Terra better."

"I wouldn't be in this situation if that jerk from New York hadn't spiked your leg sliding home that night. Or if I had settled in some other city. I hate 'what ifs', Gentry. Just drop it."

"No. We're a team, or have you forgotten that?"

"Not if we end up destroying each other." Oh, she hadn't meant to say that. Really hadn't meant even to think it.

He stiffened but didn't release her hand.

"You think I'm destroying your life? Then you really do have to let me try to fix it." His voice sounded as tight at the grip on her hands.

"I didn't mean it that way." But it was too late to retract the words. And maybe that was a good thing. Let him think she was talking about Skye's the Limit instead of Skye the woman who loved him so much she was willing to move on so her love wouldn't drag him down. "I don't want to be an obligation."

His head jerked as he turned to look at her. "An obligation? Where did you get that crazy idea?"

"I'm not your responsibility."

"I know that." Now he sounded impatient, as if explaining something to a child. "But this fix you're in? Yeah, my responsibility. Don't argue with me."

When she opened her mouth he said, "Why won't you let me take care of you? This isn't me trying to take over your life or tell you what to do. I'm not buying your building, your business, or even that fancy overpriced stove you want. I'm trying to help you out of a jam caused by me. Don't I need to take individual responsibility for my actions? I think it's called being an adult."

She looked out the side window. Tag's reflection in the glass showed he was watching her and could probably see her, but it was easier to pretend to watch Officer Brady in his cruiser than it was to look Tag in the eye.

"He can't stop me from going into my own building," she said, anxious to change the topic.

"If it's a public safety issue, he probably can."

TAG RELEASED RED's hand and wadded his fingers into a fist to keep from grabbing her and shaking some sense into her. She could be more infuriating than any other woman he'd ever met, including his mother.

The strain of the past several hours was deeply etched into her face.

Hours? Weeks. Ever since she'd arrived in New Orleans. All because of him.

"You need a lawyer," he said.

"I know," she replied. "And thank you for asking your agent to find one for me. I do appreciate your friendship. I hate taking advantage of you."

Her words, her tone, her demeanor—none of them were natural. He knew her well enough by now to know she was using her amazing internal strength to hold herself together.

Maybe she needed to fly apart in some way other than orgasm. Because he'd done a pretty good job of shattering her defenses much earlier that morning.

"What happens if you lose it?" he asked. He didn't mean merely her self-control. "What if you lose your business?"

"Then I have nothing. I am nothing."

"Oh, you're wrong about that. You're not just a caterer, babe."

"Like you're not just a baseball player?"

Why didn't she just reach between his legs and mangle his balls? It was different. He was born to play baseball. He didn't have any other skills.

She could cook. She could work in a restaurant. A fancy supermarket chain. A school cafeteria. A hospital or nursing home. She had options.

He did not.

"It's not the same thing."

"Because it's not you."

"Do you really think I'm that selfish?"

"No. If you were selfish, you wouldn't be offering to help me out. You keep bailing me out. I feel like I'm your favorite charity."

He saw her smile in the reflection of the window, but the distance couldn't mask the utter sadness behind it.

"Charity," he said, feeling suddenly wise, "begins at home."

She whirled on him. "You know, I've about had it with your platitudes. Your weird possessiveness. Your—"

Two vehicles pulled onto the street. An empty plastic bottle rattled off in the opposite direction.

Red opened her door and slid to the sidewalk. Hobbled to where Officer Brady was now standing next to his cruiser.

The second cop handed him a piece of paper. "Here's the search warrant."

"May I see that?" the occupant of the second vehicle asked. He held out his hand.

"Who are you?" Brady asked.

"Beau Ardmore. I'm Ms. Schuyler's attorney."

Tag didn't like the look of Ardmore. A generation or two earlier, the man would have been classified as a Yuppie. Slicked-back hair, natural color darkened by styling product. Lean in the way that said racquetball or some other allegedly refined sport. He probably collected rare vintages of wine that if someone actually tried to taste the stuff, would curdle his tonsils. Not that Tag was biased. Not at all. And even at this hour, Ardmore was spiffed up. All image and, Tag feared, no substance.

He and Red hobbled over to the attorney, a matched set of gimps. One of these days he'd have to get around to obtaining a handicapped parking tag for his vehicle. But not yet. He wasn't ready.

Ardmore studied the papers. "This appears in order," he said. He peered at Red over the lenses of his rimless glasses. "Ms. Schuyler?"

Red nodded. "I'll unlock the door so the officers can get in."

Tag let her limp to the door on her own. He understood that this was her business. Her livelihood. The dream that had kept her going through a lousy childhood.

She unlocked the front door. Opened it.

The reek that rolled out of the restaurant nearly knocked Tag over.

The cops immediately covered their noses and mouths.

Red gagged. Turned away and tossed her breakfast into the gutter. Tag was tempted to join her.

"What the hell is that?" Brady asked.

Ardmore was leading Red downwind of the door. Tag followed.

"Want to tell me what's going on?" Ardmore asked.

Red quickly filled him in. "Other the brick through the window and glass on the floor, everything was fine when I left last night. Officer Brady saw Tag and I leave. Tag took me to the ER because I stepped on the broken glass."

Ardmore's gaze dipped to Red's foot.

"They'll have records of the time we got there and the time we left."

"And the security on my building's underground parking lot can confirm the time we arrived at my penthouse," Tag added.

"This is all good. So what's going on?"

"I don't know," Red said. "Tag brought me over today so I could work on the Purim carnival at the JCC."

"You're catering that?" Ardmore asked. One of his eyebrows rose nearly to his hairline.

Red lifted her chin. "I'm a certified kosher caterer."

"I hope you're making kasha knish," Ardmore said. "The last caterer didn't bother with them."

Red glanced at the still open door. "I don't have a good feeling about this," she whispered.

Brady came barreling out the door and rushed to his cruiser. Red sagged.

"You need to be off that foot," Tag said, again cursing that his own injury prevented him from hauling her into his arms and to the relative comfort of his vehicle.

Ardmore strode toward Brady who was on a cell phone. Once Brady disconnected, Ardmore said something. Brady's response was short. He returned to the building and Ardmore strode toward his client.

"WHAT IS IT?" Skye didn't know this lawyer from Adam, but he was all she had at the moment.

"It appears someone butchered a pig on the premises."

If Tag hadn't caught her, she definitely would have fallen on her backside.

"A pig?" Whoever was behind this spate of vandalism was going for her jugular.

Ardmore's mouth was a grim line in his narrow face. "How much food have you already prepped for the Purim Carnival?"

"Too much." She needed to call Joel Green. Let him know what was going on.

"I was afraid of that." Ardmore's tone was as dire as his expression.

"Even if I purchase all new ingredients and begged use of the JCC's kitchen, I can't recover from this."

"You can use my kitchen again," Tag offered. Which was sweet of him, considering how much grief she'd given him the last time she moved her business into his penthouse.

"Thank you." She wasn't in the mood to explain that because his kitchen wasn't kosher, she couldn't cook for the JCC there.

"I need to call Joel Green." Her fingers shook as she pulled her phone from her pocket.

"The new director of the JCC?" Ardmore asked. "He's a putz."

"He's been very gracious while dealing with me," Skye replied.

Ardmore launched into a story about the first time he'd met Green.

"He's easy to bribe," Skye said. "He likes apricot hamantaschen."

Tag rolled his eyes.

It was too early for Green to be at his office. He was probably the kind of man who turned his cell phone off at night. Skye had to leave a message.

Several more vehicles pulled up to the building.

"We're not going to be allowed inside, are we?" she asked Ardmore.

"Nope. It's a crime scene. You have apricot hamantaschen in there? What other flavors?"

So Skye inventoried what she'd already prepared for the carnival. Doing so kept her mind off what the swelling ranks of police were doing inside her building.

Until Joel Green showed up. Of course he wouldn't return her call. Would want to see for himself.

"Beau. Skye. Gentry. What's going on?" he asked as he climbed out of his car.

"My client isn't sure," Ardmore replied. "She placed the call to you as a courtesy. She's been subjected to extreme vandalism which may or may not affect her ability to fulfill her contract for the Purim Carnival."

Joel swore.

"As I said," Ardmore replied, "she called you as a courtesy."

"This is because of the steroid story, isn't it?" Joel sounded furious. "I knew as soon as I figured out who you were that you were bad news."

Apparently Tag's agent had filled the lawyer in on everything. "My client is as much a victim of the steroid story as Tag Gentry." He sounded wonderfully pompous.

Pomposity, however, was not going to salvage the Purim Carnival. Or her business. This was it. The end. She had only the most basic insurance she could afford, which would never pay for cleanup of the magnitude suggested by the swarm of cops.

Skye looked Joel straight in the eye. "The cops said it was pig blood."

Horror replaced the fury in Joel's expression.

Skye turned to Tag, because she guessed he didn't have a clue about what going on. "I have my kosher certification. Part of kosher meat preparation is to soak the meat in salted water three times to remove the blood. And the meat has to be from a kosher animal. Pigs are not kosher."

Tag grimaced. "Using pig's blood was a twofer."

She nodded, before turning to Joel again. "Worst-case scenario, the kosher kitchen is no more and I have to toss everything I've already made and purchased. But, if I can use the facilities at the JCC for food prep—I don't want to leave you in the lurch."

Skepticism replaced the horror—the man had as many masks as a Mardi Gras parade.

"Did you say you have a kosher kitchen in the building?" Ardmore asked.

Skye nodded, still waiting for Joel to respond.

"Then this is a hate crime," Ardmore declared. "If indeed the cops are dealing with pig blood."

Joel nodded. "Right. We've been concerned about security since the election. When I found out about...the baseball connection to Skye, the board has been extremely concerned."

"Labeling this a hate crime doesn't help me fulfill my contractual obligation to the JCC. The Purim Carnival is in four days."

If Joel agreed to her plan, she was going to have to swallow her pride and ask Tag for a loan so she could purchase the supplies she'd need. She wasn't using him as a bank. He would help her. She knew that. Besides, she was desperate. She'd do almost anything to salvage this job. Who was going to care about a hate crime in South Carolina, where until recently the Confederate flag flew over the statehouse? No, she couldn't count on justice. But she could count on Tag.

Just like he could count on her to keep his secret, despite the cost to her. Like her business. But she had to try to save it without really betraying him. A heroine in one of her romance novels had once said, *Sacrificing your happiness for the happiness of the one you love is by far the truest type of love.*

Well she couldn't love him any truer than she did. At least this was baseball, the only place a sacrifice was truly appreciated.

Skye disconnect the phone call and sat on the leather love seat in Tag's living room. "Pig's blood."

They'd stayed at Skye's the Limit for several hours. Finally Tag and the lawyer suggested they wait elsewhere. The rain stopped threatening and poured down on them. It only made sense to retreat to Tag's penthouse. The lawyer accompanied them.

He was an interesting mixture of talking strategy and telling tales, most of which had nothing to do with Skye's predicament.

"There are a lot of pig farms in the area," Tag said. In other circumstances, it might have been a non sequitur.

"I think I've heard that," Skye replied.

"I've smelled it," Tag continued. "It's worse than Terra's perfume."

Terra's perfume. That was where she'd heard it. The night Terra showed up with Tag's brother.

"Didn't Terra say she was in Columbia to do a story on the pig farms?"

Tag's eyes widened. Then he shook his head. "Too messy. Terra is obsessively fastidious about her person."

"Why would you suspect her?" Ardmore asked.

So Tag and Skye explained to him what had happened in New Orleans. About the phony shipment of steroids and how Skye planned to take the materials back to Columbia to destroy. How her suitcase had been stolen during the chaos of one of the Mardi Gras parades. Yes, she'd gotten it back but hadn't discovered the incriminating documents had been stolen from the suitcase until she returned to the guesthouse. And how that was when she learned she'd also lost her phone. And the next day, an e-mail sent from Skye's phone to reporter Terra Baldwin with a photo of the packing slip for anabolic steroids, addressed to Tag, turned into the sports story of the week.

"Hmm. Do you want to press charges for defamation of character? We could subpoena phone company records to collaborate Tag's assertion that the phone wasn't in your possession in the time frame the e-mail was sent."

Skye shook her head. "I can't afford that. I can't even afford you racking up billable hours sitting here with me now."

Surprisingly, Tag agreed with her. Didn't chime in with his usual offer to pay. Even played devil's advocate. "If I didn't believe in Red's integrity, I could paint you a scenario where she faked the whole thing. All I have is her word about what happened at the Krewe d'Etat Parade. No witnesses until after the fact. She could have sent the e-mail, then planted her phone outside for Terra and Noah to find the next morning, then faked the whole *waahh I lost my phone* scenario."

Skye stared at Tag. Shocked. "I see you've given this quite a bit of thought." She couldn't keep the chill from her voice.

Tag shrugged. "I'd have to be stupid and self-destructive not to have thought about it."

"You forget one thing. The Shaneybrooks walked me home from the parade. I was never alone to plant the phone anywhere."

"You could have waited until they left. I don't know how much time elapsed between your arrival at Noah's until you made your way to the guesthouse."

The ice from her voice seeped into her throat. Spread. Plopped like an evil frog into the roiling contents of her stomach.

He hadn't believed her in New Orleans, despite defending her to Tripp Shaneybrook.

"You're absolutely right. And now I've arranged for swine slaughter in my kosher facility so I can declare bankruptcy and leave town."

"I didn't say I believed it."

She'd leave except she had nowhere else to go and no way to get there, not to mention a lack of clothes. All she had was her phone and the shorts and shirt in which she usually slept. No purse, no wallet—the cops even had the keys to her building.

"I don't know why you're being so pissy," Tag said. "I didn't even think of those things until later. My gut instinct was to trust you. To believe you. Because I do trust and believe you. I was just pointing out possible holes in your story."

Some of her tension eased. "I'm a wreck," she admitted. "My life is a wreck. I'm losing business because of the e-mail I never sent. I nearly lost the Purim Carnival because of it, and now I'm going to lose that anyway. My trash collection company cancelled my contract, and no one else will deal with me. I'm getting hate mail and all kinds of disgusting spam in my e-mail. This whole steroid fiasco was worse for me than it was for you."

"A bonus," Tag said.

"At least you can prove you've haven't been taking steroids. If you want to. Good old Hector and his pee tests. I can't prove anything."

"You can prove you're clean?" Ardmore asked. "Then why don't you?"

Tag's mouth clamped in that stubborn way Skye knew all too well.

"It doesn't matter," she said. "Even if he comes clean, I'm still the bad guy in the story. Maybe even more so it he can prove it's all a lie, because then I framed an innocent man. For all anyone knows, I'm the one who ordered the pills in Tag's name."

"Bluto," Tag said. He stopped slouching in his recliner. Narrowed his eyes at Skye. "You called Bluto from New Orleans and gave him shit for putting me on steroids. He mentioned it yesterday. Gave *me* shit about it and threatened to drop me as a client. Because *you* believed I was on steroids."

"So Bluto, who knows me, believes I'm guilty too." She didn't know why that bothered her as much as it did, but he wouldn't be getting any organic carrot cakes from her again in this lifetime.

"Actually, he doesn't." Tag sounded thoughtful. "If you were going to make a stink about it, you wouldn't have called him first."

"I guess I owe him a cake." If she ever got her kitchen back. "But don't you see? It doesn't matter. Nothing will help. Not denying the story, not marriage to you, not getting on TV and telling everyone how you can prove you're not doping—nothing. Unless Terra or Noah confesses, I'm the villain."

Officer Brady showed up at Tag's hours after Ardmore left. Hours after Red locked herself in one of the guest rooms, not wanting to be with him.

Tag wasn't happy about that, but short of going Neanderthal on her, he didn't know what to do.

He rapped on the guest room door and told her Brady wanted to speak with her.

"The damage is mainly confined to your big kitchen," Brady said.

"That's good, isn't it?" Tag asked. The kosher kitchen where she prepped all the food for Purim Carnival was smaller.

Red waved him off. "What else?" she asked Brady. "Can I get back in? I need clothes. I need my purse."

So she wasn't simply focused on her business. Maybe there was hope for them yet.

Then he noted how Brady's gaze once more took in Red's shapely legs. Naked shapely legs. Tag reminded himself her shorts, sleep shirt, and robe covered more than a swimsuit would, but knowing something didn't defuse instinct. And his instinct was to punch Officer Brady in the nose for lusting after Red.

Tag should have lent her one of his robes. It would certainly cover more than her piece of what looked like his grandmother's old bedspread.

"You can get in." Brady handed her the keys. "You probably want to call your insurance company. They have the names of businesses that clean after—messes similar to this."

Red nodded.

"Here's your copy of the police report. You'll need the number for your insurance company."

She nodded again.

He said a couple of other things, but Tag blocked out the sound of his voice. He was too busy thinking of how he could help Red.

"Don't lock yourself in the guest room again," he said after Brady finally left.

"I wasn't going to. Can you drive me home?"

She was home. He just didn't know how to make her see that.

"Of course. Then we can figure out a course of action."

She blinked at the 'we', but didn't argue.

Tag wrapped his arms around her. She felt frail to him. Beat up and vulnerable. She resisted only a fraction of what he'd expected, finally resting her head against his chest.

This felt right. Good. The way things were supposed to be between them.

He kissed the top of her head. Her hair smelled like peaches. "How's the foot feeling?"

"Hurts," she murmured.

"You probably won't be doing much of that cleaning yourself."

Her inhalation was shaky. "There's no way I can get it cleaned up myself and still meet my obligation to the JCC."

His Red was a pragmatist.

"And you can't use my kitchen."

He felt her shake her head. "My only option is the JCC's facility, and right now, I don't think Joel Green is awfully fond of me. If it wasn't so close to the carnival, he probably would have cancelled the contract as soon as we returned from New Orleans."

"His loss." Tag didn't know what else to do except show her, prove to her that he was good in a crisis. That she wasn't the only one who could be supportive. Because Red had been nothing but supportive of him since he'd first met her.

"How about a kiss for luck?" he murmured.

He felt rather than heard her chuckle. That was how they'd first met. During baseball season, when she'd catered the clubhouse meals for the players. Tag started the request as a joke—*Hey Red! How about a kiss for luck?* And when it seemed to work, became his home game ritual. Ball players were notoriously superstitious.

"Let's get something to eat before we head over there. You haven't eaten all day."

"In my pajamas?"

"We'll hit a drive-through."

TAG WAS RIGHT. She did need to eat something. Stress wasn't the only thing making her light-headed.

But fast food?

There weren't any other choices. Unless... "Aren't there leftovers from the two meals I catered for your brothers' visit?"

"Um, no." He looked slightly embarrassed. "We tend to be midnight snackers in my family. Especially when we're together."

So they stopped at a chain that had baked potatoes on the menu and ate in the parking lot.

Dusk was falling when they arrived at Skye's the Limit. They entered through the front door, as that was the only key Skye had.

The stench was as solid as a wall, maybe more solid than the partitions in the old building.

Tag's face turned an interesting shade of green. "Breathe through your mouth," he suggested.

She didn't want whatever particles hovering in the air to touch her tongue. Her taste buds might not survive. "Maybe it won't be as bad upstairs," she said.

Brady had told them the slaughtered swine carcass had been removed as evidence. Too bad the stink hadn't followed.

Skye limped to the stairs. She wanted out of her sleepwear and into jeans and a T-shirt. It was a long way up to her bedroom.

"Can you manage the climb?" Tag asked.

"Yeah."

"Maybe I'll try it too."

"It's the third floor."

He shrugged. "I'm curious."

So he followed her up the steps, leaning heavily on the railing. That worried her too. She wasn't sure if it was sturdy enough to bear Tag's weight.

When she got to the second floor, she retrieved her flip-flops.

"What's with this space?" Tag asked.

"I plan to have banquet facilities here. For company holiday parties, small weddings—that sort of thing. But that's down the road."

"You have a lot of big plans."

"I have a dream. A goal. This building is the basis for everything."

The stink faded as they made their way to the third floor.

Skye wondered how her living space looked to an outsider. Pretty bleak, she concluded. Chips of paint that had fallen from the brick walls coated the bare wooden floors. Those needed to be refinished. The space was really more of an attic than a habitat, but she didn't need much. Just a bed. A shower. A place to hang her sparse collection of clothing.

"I think," Tag said, looking around, his expression neutral, "you should stay with me until the building is secure again. Or at least until the blood and guts are cleaned up and it smells a little better. I think my nostrils are numb."

"I don't want to impose."

"Damn it, Red. When are you going to realize you are not an imposition? Maybe I have ulterior motives for wanting you at my place."

"Like wanting me in your bed?" She lifted a duffel bag from the bottom of her chifforobe. She didn't have a choice. She couldn't stay there, nor could she afford a hotel and was pretty sure her insurance wouldn't cover one. She pulled a peach-colored long-sleeved T-shirt and a pair of jeans from her bureau and went into the bathroom to change. Regular clothes felt good after being in her sleepwear all day.

"What's so wrong with wanting to make love to you?" Tag asked when she emerged.

If only it were making love.

She started stuffing things from her drawers into the duffel. Chef whites. Jeans. T-shirts. Panties and bras. Socks. "We're good together," she said. "The way we are."

The way we were.

"Damn right. If I had my way, you'd be living in the penthouse with me."

She laughed, trying to keep things light, but the sound seemed to thud to the floor like the medicine ball from grammar school gym class. "I'll stay with you for the time being."

"You don't need to sound so excited," he grumbled.

She zipped the duffel and slung it over her shoulder. "That's it for up here. I want to check the kosher kitchen—see if there's anything salvageable."

The trip down the stairs was just as laborious. Tag stopped to rest his leg on the second floor. "One thing is for sure. You get your exercise living here. Work off your cooking."

Skye found herself holding her breath as they neared the bottom of the stairs. The smell didn't mix well with the lump of burger and potato weighing down her stomach. Tag followed her to the smaller kitchen.

As Brady had said, it was relatively blood free. Unfortunately, when it came to blood, especially pig blood, relatively meant she might not be able to salvage anything.

There was nothing she wanted more to do at that moment than to give up. Surrender her dream to reality. But then she wanted to be able to hold her head up. Not only to survive but also to persevere.

She opened the freezer. The seal had kept the blood from spattering inside. The hamantaschen and mini knish were intact. She pulled out her phone to take a photo. Maybe she could convince Joel Green the food wasn't *trayf*—a Yiddish word meaning unclean.

"We should stop and pick up some air fresheners," Tag said. He sounded as if he was choking. "If we don't hurry up and get out of here, you're going to need to wash all your clothes when we get back to my place."

Skye took a few pictures. She agreed with Tag. She would need a gas mask before she could spend any length of time working there again. A call to the insurance company was definitely at the top of her agenda in the morning.

"Let's get out of here. All this blood and guts is giving me the creeps," he muttered.

Skye nodded. "I want to drive my van. I'll meet you on the street. Go out the front and make sure you lock up behind you." She handed Tag the key. Stood on tiptoe to plant a kiss on his cheek. He was being a good sport.

She slung her purse over her shoulder along with her duffel and opened the back door. For the zillionth time, she wished she had motion-detecting lights in the alley. It was full dark now. The security light over the door was out. The one functioning streetlamp at the end of the alley cast more shadows than light. She paid a little more attention to her surroundings than she normally would have. The vandalism put her on edge.

Her van was a ubiquitous plain white economy model. She'd purchased it used. Magnetized signs on the driver and passenger doors announced to the world that the van belonged to Skye's the Limit catering. As she neared the van, she saw something dark spattered on the door, obliterating the sign. She couldn't use her nose to detect what the substance was because being inside with the pig blood had neutralized her olfactory sense.

What she did know was that she was afraid to open the door. Chills spiked the hair on her arms and her nape. Something was wrong. Desperately wrong. *Trust your instincts,* someone had once told her. She fumbled for her phone. Dialed Tag.

Boom! A flash of light. The rumbling of the ground beneath her cheek.

All she knew was that she was on the pavement, sharp pebbles and maybe bits of glass from broken bottles trying to crawl inside her skin. The cool evening air had turned into an inferno, and her ears had joined her nostrils in the useless category. Even when the ground stopped shaking, her body continued to tremble.

She tried to remember how she ended up prone in the alley. At least she knew she was in the alley behind Skye's the Limit, but there was something wrong with her vision. Everything was flickering in orange tinted shadows. And her head hurt. It hurt so bad. Her knees and palms were starting to sting, too. Despite the heat licking at her body, her bones were cold. So cold. Her teeth chattered.

Then Tag was in her face. His mouth was open, the rest of his features twisted in with horror. Streaks of liquid fire delineated his cheeks. Why was he wearing a mask? Mardi Gras was a week ago. Purim wasn't until the weekend. His hands, his big calloused fingers and palms stroked her cheek with a gentleness that belied their size. She didn't understand why his lips were moving if he wasn't talking. His behavior only added to her confusion, increasing her headache. She closed her eyes. That helped. Apparently she was nauseated, too, but that also subsided a little when she closed her eyes.

Sleep. That was what she wanted to do. What her body craved.

Tag was in his SUV when he heard the explosion. When the remaining windows blew out of Skye's the Limit. When fire lit up the night... "Skye!"

The howl came straight from his soul. Cursing his lameness as he hadn't done since he'd missed catching in the World Series, he did his best to rush to the alley. His best wasn't good enough. Not anymore. He dialed 9-1-1 but didn't waste his breath trying to explain anything. He had to get to Red. He had to find her. Had to make certain she was okay. There were no windows on the back of the building. But had she gotten out?

Then he saw her pale orange T-shirt in the darker, orange-stained shadows. She was stretched out on the ground near her van. And she wasn't moving.

He howled again and dropped his phone. "Red!"

Kneeling on the broken blacktop next to her, ignoring the screaming in his leg because he could put up with a little pain—he prayed Red was okay. She blinked at him, reflections of the flames flickering in her eyes. But she didn't say anything. Didn't move, except to close her eyes.

What if something else in the building blew? But he didn't dare move her. Didn't know how badly she was injured. If her neck was broken or her skull fractured. If she was paralyzed.

He picked up one limp hand. One icy, flaccid hand. He searched for a pulse in her wrist and found one. A strong one. Half-remembered prayers from his half-baked religious education came back to him. Mindless phrases, repeated from a brain too numb to string together a coherent sentence. He prayed to any deity who would listen. "Please be okay. Let her be okay."

Finally. Sirens in the distance, gradually becoming louder, shrieking in the night, echoing the anguish he was trying to contain. He inhaled but started coughing. His eyes watered as much from the smoke as from emotion. And his sense of smell was coming back, but nothing he could define.

Then footsteps. "Hello? Anyone back here?" A cop with a flashlight.

"Over here!" Tag called, then coughed again. "She's hurt. You have to help her."

"Was there anyone else in the building?"

"No. She needs an ambulance. Call for help."

What had been a deserted alley became a hub of activity. Fire trucks, hoses, firefighters. An ambulance. EMTs with a backboard. Red groaned as she was strapped on to it.

That meant she could feel, that she was alive. For now.

He was loaded onto a stretcher and into a separate ambulance.

THURSDAY, MARCH 9

The ceiling had a stain shaped like the head of a famous cartoon mouse. It wasn't as if Skye had anything else, much less anything better to do than stare at the ceiling. The pattern of dots on the tiles resembled a peace sign. Peace. Yeah. Right.

"How are you doing?" Tag asked, as he'd been doing almost hourly since she'd regained consciousness.

"The same." Her hearing had finally returned. Apparently loud noises caused sudden but temporary deafness in some situations. Her sense of smell was back too. With a vengeance. She wanted nothing more than to scrub her hair and skin in a scalding shower, but the good folks at the hospital weren't being very cooperative. They wanted her to rest. In small doses. Tag volunteered to wake her up every hour. Except she wasn't sleeping. For many reasons, starting with she couldn't stand the smell of herself—singed hair, pig blood mixed with smoke, maybe even dog doo thrown in for good measure. Yeah, her stink was the immediate reason she couldn't sleep.

But there were others. The explosion. At least, that was what the cops and Tag had told her. Skye's the Limit had blown sky high. She'd lost everything, even what she'd packed in the duffel to take to Tag's house. It had blown off her body when the building went up. The ambulance ran over it. A couple of times. Then the hospital cut off her jeans and T-shirt to treat her for possible burns both from the fire and from sliding across the alley. Not that she remembered that part. She didn't remember much at all.

And when she wasn't trying to remember what had happened, she wanted to vomit. Wished she'd been inside the building when whatever happened had happened. Because pig blood wasn't the worst thing that could have happened to her.

Tag perched in the chair next to her bed and reached for her hand. Played with the ring he'd shoved on her finger.

She didn't have the energy to deal with his misplaced guilt. His still palpable fear. His obsession that she speak to him. Him.

At least he had the sense not to talk about—

She wished she *could* sleep. So much for a concussion.

Her new best friend, Officer Brady, stopped by at about four in the morning. "The fire is out."

"So?" The single syllable lent itself nicely to croaking.

"So the fire investigator will be able to start nosing around as soon as things cool off a bit."

What good would an investigation into the shell of her life do? The insides, the guts, her sweat equity—gone. All gone.

And the crazy shaking started again. In her stomach. Her eyes. Her teeth. No one said anything, so maybe they didn't notice.

No matter who or what had caused the explosion, an investigation couldn't bring back anything. Couldn't change her loss.

"There might have been a gas leak." Brady continued. "Power company records show some issues last fall."

"That was the stove. I replaced it."

"No one could have smelled a gas leak," Tag added. "The burners and ovens on the stove could all have been blowing out gas full throttle, no one would even know it."

Yes, she knew she was lucky she hadn't been killed or even more seriously injured. Yes, she was grateful Tag hadn't been hurt either. Well, hurt worse than he'd been. He'd done some additional damage to his leg trying to get to her. He didn't know she knew. But how could she miss his worsened limp? A hoarsely whispered telephone conversation with his doctor while Tag thought she slept?

So now that was at her doorstep too. Just about the only thing she hadn't done to mess up his life was to have been the one to spike him in his knee last October. Great track record for someone who loved him. Now marriage was really out of the question. If she married him, he'd end up dead.

"Have you contacted your insurance company yet?" Brady asked.

"I don't have a phone." Even she could hear the dullness, the apathy in her tone. If she ever recovered from this disaster, everything was going to be handled the old-fashioned way. Hard copies of phone contacts, contracts, menus, price quotes. But thinking about a future drove spikes of pain into her skull, so she stopped. Thinking. Feeling. Hoping. Giving a damn.

"Your new one will be here after the phone store opens," Tag said. "Don't argue."

No, she wouldn't argue. Until she could figure out how to get back on her feet again, she was going to be a kept woman. She didn't have a choice. She didn't even have a pair of underwear, clean or otherwise. Since Tag was so anxious to take care of her, she'd let him. She'd go along with the faux engagement.

Until she could pull herself up again.

Fortunately she was numb. She could zombie her way through this latest disaster. Even if she didn't want to.

"And I'm having Macy's send over some clothes in your size," Tag continued.

"Thank you."

He narrowed his eyes. "That's it? Thank you?"

"I can't argue with kindness."

"*Kindness?*"

"It's not kindness? Then what is it? Tell me, so I know how to react."

He toyed with the ring on her left hand but didn't say anything else.

Brady cleared his throat. "We don't have a report number to give you yet, but as soon as we—"

"Don't worry about it."

"She understands," Tag corrected. "And appreciates your efforts."

Oh, he was so good at the spin. Of course, players were coached not only in game fundamentals but in public relations.

Tag was really getting worried. Red wasn't talking. Oh, he could force a syllable out of her now and then, and she was free with those dreadful *thank yous* when something like new jeans and T-shirts showed up. But it was as if she wasn't there. Not in the room with him. Maybe not in her body. Okay, she'd taken a pretty bad knock on the head when the building blew, but Tag's gut insisted her withdrawal was more, was worse than that.

Especially when Terra showed up.

"Who let the press in here?" Tag lurched from his chair, fully intending to toss Terra out on her ass.

Terra held up her hand. "I'm not here in a professional capacity." She looked like hell. The dark blue circles under her eyes looked deep enough to swim in. "I'm here as a friend."

"You lost any right to call me a friend when you framed Red for breaking that fake news story about me on steroids."

He waited for Red to jump in. Back him up. But her eyes were closed. Her chest barely rose and fell. She scared him.

"I never thought—"

"You never have thought." Tag nearly spat at her.

"No one was supposed to get hurt!"

Everything inside Tag went perfectly still, including, he thought, his heart.

"What do you know about the explosion?" He spoke as softly as he could, because he was still in control.

Terra twisted her fingers. He didn't think he'd ever seen her as distressed as she was. She blinked. Several times. Rapidly. Caught her bottom lip between her teeth.

Tag pulled his phone from his pocket. "I know a police officer who wants to talk to you." His voice was harsh, his tone brutal. He dialed the number Brady had given him.

"She wasn't supposed to be there," Terra whispered. "Neither were you, but she—she wasn't supposed to be there."

"It was my home." Red finally spoke. Opened her eyes. "Where else would I be?"

"Oh, Skye, I'm so sorry. I'm going to the police after I leave here. I just needed to see that you're really going to be okay."

"You're not going anywhere," Tag growled. He hoped he didn't throttle her before the cops arrived.

"Why?" Red asked. "What did I ever do to you?"

"You took Tag."

Tag couldn't believe what he was listening to. Brady finally answered his phone. "Better get over to the hospital. Terra Baldwin is here confessing to everything."

"Everything?" Terra shook her head. "Not me. But I know who."

"Drake Dixon. That's a no-brainer. What's wrong? Now that he's in deep shit for gambling he's not rich enough for you, so you wanted to come crawling back to my bed?"

"It's not like that."

"I don't see how it could be anything but that. Except what makes you think you were even missed in my bed?"

"You were never as nice to me as you are to Skye."

"She's a nicer person."

"I have a career I'm trying to build."

"So does Red. And you fucked her over big-time."

"Not me. Not only me. Drake. He was really pissed about the Halloween video."

"Because if I release it, the world will see what a small dick he has? It's my video, not Red's. Why go after her?"

"Not that part. He's worried you recorded the guests. And some of them wouldn't...like being recorded."

"I don't blame them, but I'm not into porn."

"You don't understand. There were some...dangerous people there. People Drake owed money to."

"The gambling," Tag said, finally understanding. "Mob? But why piss me off? Why piss off Red?"

"To destroy your credibility should you ever decide to go public with the recording. And now I think I want my lawyer," Terra whispered.

"I think that's probably a real good idea."

"WAIT." SKYE STRUGGLED to sit upright. The top of her head felt as if it was bursting open. "I want to make a deal."

"You what?" Tag asked.

"I want to make a deal," Skye repeated.

"You have a head injury. Your brain is scrambled. You're not thinking straight."

"Would you say the same thing if I agreed to marry you?"

"Marry her?" Terra whispered.

"Is that part of the deal?" Tag countered at the same time.

Skye ignored him. Focused her throbbing attention on Terra. "A deal, Terra. If you admit, on national television, that you and Noah set me up, I won't press charges."

"That won't stop me from pressing them," Tag said.

"Stay out of this, Gentry." Skye thought she sounded a lot stronger than she felt. But Tag stopped talking. "If you'll admit you purposely smeared my name in that damned e-mail, I won't press charges."

Terra's mouth opened, as if she were trying to take in more oxygen. "How can I trust you?"

"That's your problem," Skye replied.

"How's your head?" Tag asked as he opened the door to his penthouse.

"I have a headache," Skye admitted. "They told me I would for a while." She trailed Tag inside, limping almost as badly as he did. She headed straight to the guest bathroom. "I'm taking a shower," she told him.

"Not alone, you're not."

Skye inhaled deeply, which only made her head hurt worse. "I'm not in the mood to…"

Tag hooked an arm around her waist, halting her progress. "That's okay. I can be with you without making love."

Skye flinched. There was that phrase again.

"But there is no way I'm letting you in the shower alone with a head injury. It's not going to happen." His tone was rough. He steered her toward his room.

"I stink," she said.

"We both do."

"My new clothes stink too."

"Yep. You don't need clothes to shower or sleep in. I've seen you naked. You look fabulous naked. You don't need to worry about me. Nothing will happen unless you want it to."

That was part of the problem. Wanting something to happen between them, no matter how often her brain told her heart and her girl bits that staying involved in a physical relationship with Tag was only going to be a disaster.

"I'm steady enough on my feet. Really, I just need some privacy."

His expression darkened, as if he didn't quite trust her. "What? You've already called your insurance agent and Beau Ardmore. Were you planning to call your guy at the JCC to tell him his food went up in flames? He probably already knows."

Damn. She'd forgotten about Joel. But that wasn't the reason she didn't want him around. "Are you going to hover?"

"Until the docs tell me not to."

"I need time to grieve, and I don't feel like I can with you hanging over me."

"Grieve? It was a building, Red. I mean, I know it was your building. It housed your dream, but it was still just a building. There are other buildings. There are even other cities. Skye's the Limit isn't that building. It's you, and you're pretty much unhurt. That's the important thing."

The emotion she thought had been gutted out of her along with Skye's the Limit staged its own explosion. "Just a building? See, you don't understand. Everything I have worked for is gone. Just...gone. The insurance can't replace everything in the structure. The insurance can't replace the jobs that were cancelled because of the steroid story. I've lost everything. Even the clothes on my back."

The tears she wanted to shed in the shower burst from her, along with sobs, loud and messy.

Red forgot one important thing: him.

Against his better judgment, Tag let her shower alone. He figured she needed a pity party. Too bad she hadn't come out and said it. But he got it. He'd been holding too many of his own lately.

Hector Michaud had laid it out for him—he was never going to play behind the plate of a major league baseball game again. Maybe it was time to...accept the unacceptable.

No one ever promised him life would be fair. Yeah. He'd had time to adjust. Not enough time, but time. Red was still raw. And she could rebuild her business.

And the first step to doing that was fulfilling her contract with the Columbia Jewish Community Center. Because honoring that meant she still had pride. Everybody needed pride. Otherwise, they couldn't keep going.

Tag used the time Red was in the shower to make a few phone calls. "My woman is in trouble." So what if he didn't tell people his woman was the one they all believed betrayed him. All any of them needed to know was that his woman needed his help, and he was pulling strings all along the eastern seaboard to get it for her.

Even a couple of former teammates, still in spring training, helped.

Red cried for a long time, but now that he understood that she wept for her losses, he let her be. Was even a little jealous that she could vent like that. He left his maroon paisley silk robe on the back of the bathroom door for her.

When she finally emerged, about an hour later, her face was red and chafed looking. Puffy eyes. Bowed head.

"Want something to eat?" Tag asked. He figured they could order in Chinese or a pizza or something. But Red shook her head and kept walking toward the kitchen.

"I'm warning you. There's nothing here for you to cook."

She kept walking. Opened his fridge. Pulled out a bottle of water. Her hands were shaking so badly she couldn't twist off the top. Tag took it from her and did the honors. Then he grabbed her hand and led her to the living room. Sat on the love seat and pulled her down beside him before relinquishing her water. She was probably dehydrated from crying so much.

"I made some calls while you were in the shower."

She wasn't relaxed, but his statement stiffened her like a bat. He didn't let go of her.

"What you need to do now," he continued, "is call your JCC guy. Joe. Let him know you're still catering the festival."

"Impossible."

"Not impossible. I made phone calls to some former teammates who are in New York now. Yeah, it's gonna cost me, but

I'd rather spend my money on you than let it sit around gather dust."

He braced himself for her inevitable argument.

She said nothing.

"I called a couple of kosher delis and ordered a crap load of kosher holiday food. It's all being expressed to Columbia tomorrow. You are *not* going to break your contract with the JCC."

She averted her face. Her sweet, sweet face. "Thank you."

He barely heard her.

"You said you lost everything. But you're wrong. You still have me."

"I don't have you. We're friends with benefits. Fuck buddies."

He hated the way she dismissed what was between them. "Is that all I am to you? A cock?"

She shook her head but wouldn't look him in the eye.

"Look at me and tell me I am not just a dick for you." His anger refused to behave and sneaked into his voice. "Tell me you don't love me. Then I'll call you a liar, we'll fight a little, then have make up sex."

She said nothing.

His brothers had told him he was in love with Red. All he knew was that he couldn't stand the thought of her being with anyone else. And last night. The explosion. When he'd thought she might have still been inside. He'd never known such terror in his life.

Maybe Hunter and Coop were right. He knew he wanted to marry her because he liked having her around. He liked the way she was always on his side. He liked looking at her. Watching TV with her. Watching her cook.

"You're going to make me say it first? I'm a guy. I don't do the emotion thing very well."

He inhaled deeply. If having to tell her would get her to marry him, he'd say the damned words. "I love you, Red. That's why I want to marry you. Not because of Marty or anything else. I want to marry you because I want you with me for the rest of my life. Oh, hell, I can't even imagine the rest of my life without you."

"Baseball. You can't imagine the rest of your life without baseball. You still talk like you're going back to the big leagues."

Yeah, she knew him down to his soul.

He inhaled deeply before replying. "I know I'm the man who loves you. The rest of it—I'll figure it out. And if I start wandering into bullshit, you'll call me on it. I need you to call me on it. Because maybe I lost my career, but I have you. You lost your building, but you have me. That's the way it works, Red. That's how a team works."

"So now you've decided to distract yourself from the rest of your life by being in love me with me. Great."

He hated the tone of her voice. He'd spilled his guts, laid out his soul to her, and she was dissing him.

Her face colored a little. "I've been a little in love with you since the first home game of last season."

Relief. Okay. He could deal. "Then what's the problem?"

An attempted smile twisted her face as she curled into the corner of the love seat. If he didn't know better, he might think she was trying to make herself smaller and avoid contact with him. "I don't think I could stand being in love with you and going through the motions when all I'd be moving toward is emptiness once your attention wanders or I don't meet your expectations. I did that with my father. Not willing to go through it again."

"What part of I love you don't you understand?" She was starting to piss him off.

"Come on. I was there when your agent told you the best way to show the world I didn't really send that e-mail about the steroids to Terra was for you to marry me." She winced.

He wanted nothing more than to wrap his arms around her and hold her. Kiss her until she forgot that telephone conversation. Until she said, *Yes. I'll marry you.*

"Yeah. Okay. But I didn't dismiss it out of hand, did I? Nope. Because I really like the idea of being married to you. Because I, you know. Love you."

He'd said it. Again. The world didn't come to an end. But Red didn't scoot across the leather cushions and melt in his arms either.

"Look. I'm here. I'm your kept woman until I can figure out what to do. Can't we just leave it at that?" She sounded desperate and unhappy and helpless.

He hated all three. She was admired, cherished, and loved.

"I don't want to leave it," he said. "I want forever with you."

"Don't." She choked on the word.

"Don't what? Be in love with you? Too late, Red." He brushed a tight curl off her cheek. Let it coil around his finger. "So if I love you and you love me, we ought to get married. I'm not joking around. We ought to get married and get out of town. I can call Tripp Shaneybrook and see if his offer to work at his summer camp is still good. It's not as if I need the money, and I am a damned good catcher. I can work with those kids. Cooperstown probably has restaurants where you can find work. We could get out of here during the worst of the summer heat. What do you say? We can get our license tomorrow. Find a JP or go down to city hall. Unless you want fancy."

He knew his Red. She wouldn't want fancy.

"Maybe we could start our family right off too. How many kids do you want? At least two. I'm firm on that. Didn't you hate being an only child?"

Her lips parted. Her eyes lost some of the vacant glaze they'd worn since the explosion. "You're serious."

"About loving you? Never more serious about anything in my life." He meant it. Every syllable. It was a relief to admit his feelings. He wasn't a hearts-and-flowers kind of guy, but Red already knew that about him. Loved him anyway. Thank God, she loved him anyway.

Red lunged into his arms. He held her tight. "So, are you going to marry me or what?"

Her answer was muffled against his chest, but it was a sound as sweet as horsehide against an ash bat. "Yes."

SUNDAY, MARCH 12

"**I** miss your apricot hamantaschen," Joel Green said. Dressed as a king, he stood next to Skye in the gymnasium of the Jewish Community Center and watched a circle of dancers kicking it up to the music from the klezmer band.

"What is that music the band is playing?" Tag asked.

"Klezmer. It's sort of like Jewish jazz." Joel tapped his foot and smiled at the dancers gyrating in front of the dais.

Tag shuddered. "I feel like I'm at Mardi Gras again. What is it about jazz, kings, and queens?"

"The Purim story is about a king and his queens." Joel smiled at the crown on Skye's head. "Don't Skye and I make a lovely couple?"

"No," Tag snarled. He looped his arm through hers. "Red is taken."

Joel laughed. "I can see that."

"The only difference I see is no booze here, as opposed to the free-flow in New Orleans," Tag said.

Joel's smile faded. "People are supposed to get so intoxicated they can't tell the hero from the villain, but this is a family event. And with the current political climate, we need to be more vigilant. Threats and hate crimes are on the rise. As you should know, people feel more comfortable venting their hatred these days."

"Yeah. I've seen some of Red's nasty messages."

Skye's face was hot under her Queen Esther mask. She felt odd, not wearing chef whites, but Tag had insisted that since she hadn't cooked the food, she not be there as a chef. He'd hired a couple of people to oversee the reheating of the food. The feast was his donation to the center. Skye didn't even really need to be present, but she felt she needed to show Joel and the people who had put their trust in her that she wasn't going to back down. In the Purim story, the queen had saved her people. In this case, the king, her king, stepped up to do the deed.

The gymnasium was filled with kids in repurposed Halloween costumes and adults dressed as kings, queens, and even the villain of the Purim story in odd-looking three-cornered hats.

But the queens were who fascinated Skye. Mardi Gras had been all about the king. Here, it seemed, the emphasis was on the queen. She said as much to Joel.

"Two queens. Vashti, who refused to pander to the king and was executed, making the way for Esther, who seduced the king into saving the Jews from being annihilated. Haman, the villain, cast lots to determine the day he planned to wipe out the Jews, but Esther stopped him. Purim means lots."

"Lots?"

"An ancient version of dice. It's a form of gambling."

Skye lifted her mask to her face to hide her expression. Gambling. Didn't it just figure. At least Tag had turned over the Halloween video to the feds, who were happy to have something else to use in pressuring Drake Dixon about the illegal gambling. Apparently he hung out with some pretty bad hombres.

Tag pulled his phone from his pocket and scowled at the screen. "Excuse me. I need to take this call." He held the phone to his ear as he exited the gym.

"Now that the truth has come out about Terra Baldwin and the phony e-mail, are you going to reopen your business?" Joel asked.

"Probably not. I don't have a building. And I'd rather not discuss this today." Even if the lump in her throat would let her.

"Of course. So have you and Tag set a date?"

"Soon," she replied. She still had problems wrapping her mind around Tag's declaration of love. He was so vital, so full of life. She was just a glorified cook, happiest when squeezing vegetables and hanging out in a kitchen. "When we do, it will be just Tag and me and a judge."

"No fairy-tale wedding?"

"I don't believe in fairy tales."

"What? You're not getting your happily ever after?" Joel's mock shock was amusing to watch. "I have to believe in happily ever after." He waved his hand at the shrieking children in their bouncy houses, the masked kings and queens and oddly hatted dancers in front of the stage, at the klezmer band. "But happily ever after takes work. It takes perseverance. My people—they've endured a lot. That's why we celebrate our survival. Purim is all about happily ever after. We make it so." He smiled. "Just some food for thought."

She hadn't considered that aspect of the story.

His gaze shifted past her shoulder. "And here comes your king."

She turned. Tag was threading his way through the crowd. A couple of kids, shrieking with laughter, knocked into him, but he didn't seem to notice.

"That was Tripp Shaneybrook," he said when he reached her.

Oh, no. What else could possibly go wrong for them?

"He has a problem and was wondering if you could call him."

"Me?" What in the world could Tripp Shaneybrook want with her? She wasn't even sure he liked her. Not that it mattered. She could get along with him for a summer if it helped Tag.

Tag handed her his phone. "Excuse us, Joel." He snatched the crown off Joel's head before leading Skye out of the gym, down the hall to another hall, where the din wasn't as raucous.

"Look, if this is about you going to Cooperstown for the summer, that's your decision."

"Just call him." He yanked the mask from her face, crumpled it, then tossed it over his shoulder. "But first, a kiss for luck." He pulled her close and for a minute or two, she forgot all about calling Tripp.

When Tag finally released her, she scrolled through his recent call log and pressed Tripp's number.

He must have been waiting for her call, because he answered right away. "Tag?"

"Skye," she corrected. "Tag said you wanted to speak to me."

"I do. Thanks for getting back to me so quickly. The cook I had lined up for this summer's session backed out on me. I'm looking for someone who can teach these future major league stars about good sports nutrition now, so that eating right becomes a habit for them. Any suggestions?"

She whirled to look at Tag, who was grinning at her. She grinned back.

"It doesn't pay much, but room and board are included," Tripp continued. "Tag said you might know someone."

"Tag is right," she said, as she reached for his hand.

Tag planted the king's crown on his head, then wrapped his arms around her waist.

"Where do I send my résumé?"

I hope you enjoyed Tag & Skye's story.

For up-to-date information on all my books, please subscribe to my newsletter.

EXCERPT: CATCHER INTERFERENCE (TAG & SKYE PART 1)

October 20, Game 7 National League Championship Series

Tucker Alexander Gentry, known throughout the baseball universe as Tag, squatted behind home plate. His thigh muscles burned. He glared at the pitcher on the mound.

The entire season had come down to this moment. Game seven of the National League Championship Series. Top of the ninth inning. Two outs. The Columbia Gems were up by one, and Tag meant to keep the score that way. The tying run was on second base—some cocky wiseass New York had recently called up from Triple-A for the postseason. The go-ahead run was on first.

And Adam Chrestler, the Gems' closing pitcher, was shaking off Tag's signals. The oversize digital scoreboard played stupid cartoon graphics behind Chrestler's head. The ballpark was so silent Tag thought he heard the hot dog vendor on the third-base side of the stadium scouring his grill.

Tag thrust his hand between his splayed thighs and flashed the sign for a slider. *Do not pitch a fastball.* Chrestler's slider was working. And the batter at the plate could knock a fastball out of the park.

If that happened, the Gems would hang up their cleats until spring. If not, the team would go to the World Series. Only one out away.

Don't think ahead. One game at a time.

If Chrestler threw a fastball, Tag would personally break a couple of the pitcher's fingers.

Chrestler released the ball. The hitter swung. The bat met the ball—loud as a firecracker—but not with the distinctive sound only made by the sweet spot on a maple bat connecting with cowhide. The batter had gotten under the pitch. Long fly ball. Leisurely sailing toward right field. The sole shooting star against the black backdrop of the nighttime sky.

The right fielder adjusted his cup and positioned his body for the catch. The play should have resulted in an easy out, but the ball smacked his glove before it bobbled to the grass.

The fans groaned, but Tag barely heard them. He focused on the punk who tagged up at second and headed for third. Tag threw off his mask and readied himself to protect home plate. Yep. The New York third-base coach was waving the punk home.

Shit, he was fast.

Tag stood directly behind the plate, silently cursing the rule change that prevented him from blocking the base. He wasn't taking any chances the out would be overturned because he'd messed up. Because he was going to make the out. Ensure his team would go to the World Series.

The ball rocketed in from right field. Punk's teeth flashed in a cocky grin the second before he went into his slide.

Tag stretched himself to catch the ball that was zooming toward him. The punk was sliding. Dust and chalk from the base path were like a jet contrail pluming behind him.

The ball landed in Tag's mitt, stinging his palm ever so slightly. He lunged forward, twisted ever so slightly, and tagged Punk's foot before it touched the base. The ump called the out.

Punk's cleats connected with the back of Tag's right knee where his leg guards didn't cover. Retracted ever so slightly, and then slammed the spot anew with the full force of Punk's body behind it.

It didn't matter. The game was over. The Columbia Gems had won the National League Pennant and were World Series bound.

Tag's teammates burst from the dugout and jumped him. Pounded his back. Danced around home plate. Fireworks exploded in the no-man's land behind the scoreboard, and a sulfuric stench from the gunpowder wafted into the stadium.

Tag's throat was dry from the billowing dust and all the whooping. He couldn't wait to get into the clubhouse and pop open the champagne management had on ice for just this occasion. It was sure going to taste mighty fine.

His teammates finally decided to let him up. He tried to stand.

His first clue something was wrong was the way his right leg wouldn't support him. The second indication was the pain that stole his breath and a sense of wetness. He hadn't been doused with the water bucket—that honor was reserved for the manager—so he looked down. And nearly puked.

CLICK HERE TO PURCHASE

EXCERPT: NO DOUBLES DEFENSE (Tag & Skye Part 2)

Wednesday, February 22 – Krewe of Druids Parade

Tucker Alexander Gentry—Tag to the baseball world—rented a red sports car at Armstrong International Airport and plugged the address his former teammate had provided into his phone.

God it felt good to be out of the wheelchair and independently mobile. Weeks without being able to walk, much less drive, were behind him. He still faced months of physical therapy, though. His last visit with the team doctor had sucked. Prognosis: Tag would miss the whole upcoming season.

If he ever got his hands on that punk from New York... The league could fine the little bastard who had plowed cleats-first into Tag's leg all they wanted, suspend the son of a bitch for a couple of games, or ban him for life like Shoeless Joe or Pete Rose. Didn't matter. No disciplinary action could give Tag back the World Series he'd missed. That theft burned worse than missing the spring training currently in session or sitting out the entire upcoming season.

So when Noah Nash, former pitching great for the Columbia Gems, had invited Tag to New Orleans for Mardi Gras, Tag had jumped at the chance. Figuratively.

Tag concentrated on the unfamiliar traffic patterns instead of on what the hell he was going to do if he couldn't play baseball again. Noah had said he might have something for him. There were only so many broadcasting positions, only so many coaching and scouting jobs—but hundreds of retired players. Pathetic men who were lost without a stadium or team to define them. Tag vowed he would never join their ranks.

The rest of the Gems were at spring training while Tag had been stuck in Columbia. Stuck and feeling sorry for himself. He should have been in Florida with the rest of the guys. Red was.

And if he couldn't be with his team, he ought to be able to do something else. Bungee jumping. Cave diving. *Something.* He was climbing the walls when he should have been rock climbing. Except his contract prevented him from doing anything that might endanger his rehab. If Terra, his currently off-again girlfriend, had been around, she could have amused him. But Terra was waiting for some volcano on some Pacific island to erupt. And they were off again. Probably permanently.

And Red? She was his new best friend. Who came with benefits. Came with— He could list a hundred ways she came and a hundred more ways he wanted to try. But Red was the team caterer and had been summoned to spring training along with the rest of the Gems.

So Noah's hint of a future career only sweetened the New Orleans vacation concept.

Once Tag got off the highway and into the city improper—and New Orleans in February was definitely improper—he ran into traffic issues. Although Fat Tuesday wasn't for another six days, the frenzied city throbbed with its Carnival celebration. Parades closed blocks of some streets the phone app told him to use. Costumed pedestrians clustered in inconvenient spots, where automobiles became intruders and had to yield to the citizens and tourists.

Everyone looked as if they were having a good time, something Tag hadn't experienced in too long. Except for some increasingly rare interludes with Red.

Red. Celeste "Skye" Schuyler. Owner of Skye's the Limit Catering. Damn it, he was trying not to think about her. The team had hired her to feed him while he'd been laid up. Once his cast had come off, she'd no longer made house calls. And with the cessation of house calls came the end of booty calls.

Tag missed her. He was loath to admit it, even to himself, but he'd grown fond of their sparring. All the things he'd ever heard about feisty redheads were true. At least, in her case. Just thinking about her had his cock twitching.

ALSO BY MJ COMPTON

CONTEMPORARY SPORTS (BASEBALL) ROMANCE

COLUMBIA GEMS BASEBALL ROMANCES

MISSING THE SIGNS – A second chance with the sexy base-ball player who ghosted me seven years ago? Let me count the "no ways".

HIT BY HIS PITCH – I was abandoned. Stranded. Broke. Until the playboy pitcher came in for the save.

CATCHER INTERFERENCE: TAG & SKYE PART 1 – One injured catcher. One sizzling caterer. A torrid post-season game neither can afford to lose.

NO DOUBLES DEFENSE: TAG & SKYE PART 2 – What's

an injured catcher to do when spring training starts without him? Losing himself in the decadence of Mardi Gras seems like a good start.

BATTING CLEANUP: TAG & SKYE PART 3 – Baseball may be the only place in life where a sacrifice is really appreciated, but catcher Tag Gentry never expected Skye Schuyler to risk everything for him.

SHIFTER- BASEBALL MASHUP NOVELLA

Shifting Home – The only shift baseball star Spike Peters knows is when players realign their defensive positions on the field. But when the most attractive woman he's ever encountered starts babbling about shifting, full moons, fated mates, and—worst of all—forever, the fastest runner in the game's first instinct is to run—straight to her bed.

SHIFTER ROMANCE

Toke Lobo & the Pack Series

MOONLIGHT SERENADE-Werewolves working for the government? Reporter Delilah Tenney must choose:the story of a lifetime or a lifetime of love.

"Compton's debut is a gripping, sexy as hell, page turner of a werewolf novel not for the faint hearted!" ~ NY Times Bestselling Author Maggie Shayne.

AND JERICHO BURNED- Lucy Callahan will do anything to save her sister, even if that means marrying a stranger. Even if that stranger is an undercover government agent out to destroy the cult holding her sister hostage. Even if that stranger is a . . . werewolf.

A Night Owl Reviews Reviewer Top Choice.

OMEGA MOON RISING- One desperate woman intent on escape. One brash werewolf determined to deny his DNA. Until his destiny becomes her deliverance.

A Night Owl Reviews Reviewer Top Choice.

Service for Sanctuary Series

BETRAYED BY THE MOON – Service for sanctuary–that was the werewolves' deal for over 200 years. Now the government is changing the rules, leaving Ethan Calhoun fighting for the only way of life he's ever known— and Selena Wolfe fighting for her life.

BEWARE OF THE MOON – One-night stands don't turn into forever unless you happen to pick-up a werewolf. She thought the hook-up was just another one-and-done. He knew she was his one-and-only. But when his mission unlocks the treacheries of her past, they are forced to put aside their differences as they battle for their lives.

BESIEGED BY THE MOON – Fated soul mates. She's a werewolf assassin in heat on a mission. He's a werewolf EMT and the father of her future children. What could possibly go wrong?

About the Author

MJ Compton grew up near Cardiff, New York, a place best known for its giant—a hoax so successful, P.T. Barnum duplicated it. The tale of the "petrified man" convinced MJ that inventing stories could be a career.

Although her 30 years working in local television included such highlights as being bitten by a lion, preempting a US President for a college basketball game, giving a three-time world champion boxer a few black eyes, and meeting her husband, MJ never lost her dream of creating her own stories.

MJ still lives in upstate New York with her husband. Music and cooking are two of her passions, and she enjoys baseball, college basketball, and sitting on her patio on summer nights to count lightning bugs, but she's primarily focused on writing.